MADE IN L.A.

MADE IN L.A.

CHASING THE ELUSIVE DREAM

MADE IN L.A.
Chasing the Elusive Dream

SECOND ANNUAL ANTHOLOGY

Cover design by Allison Rose

Visit Made in L.A. Writers online at
www.madeinlawriters.com

ISBN: 978-0-9987607-5-9
Library of Congress Control Number: 2019936871

Published by Resonant Earth Publishing
on behalf of
MADE IN L.A. WRITERS
P.O. Box 50785
Los Angeles, CA 90050

CONTENTS

Introduction

INTRODUCTION

When we first came together in 2017 under the Made in L.A. banner, Angelenos got excited. They asked us if our stories were set in L.A.

Our responses were mixed: some of them were, others weren't.

This set us on a path to create stories that would appeal to local readers. We couldn't do it alone; we had to reach out to our writer friends to compile and curate a collection of stories set in and inspired by Southern California. Thus, *Made in L.A.: Stories Rooted in the City of Angels* was born.

When we debuted this anthology at the 2018 L.A. Festival of Books, it was our turn to get excited. Halfway through the second day, we sold out of all copies of the anthology! We were overwhelmed and humbled by the enthusiasm readers had for our stories.

Spurred on by this win, we reached out to local booksellers, who supported us by stocking our anthology in their stores. Two bookstores — Stories Books & Café and Book Show — hosted readings for the anthology as well, and contributing authors participated at these events. We're excited to have these new connections and would like to extend special thanks to Book Show, Stories Books & Café, Skylight Books, the Last Bookstore, and DIESEL, A Bookstore for their ongoing support.

As 2019 approached, we rallied ourselves for the next challenge: Volume Two. We brainstormed about preparing for a second anthology at local pubs, looking for inspiration from each other (as well as from our beverages). Our emphasis, this time, would be on the hopes and dreams of Angelenos, as well as the dark forces at work in our conscious and unconscious lives. We batted about phrases such as "living the dream," " in search of the dream," "California dreams," and "mosaic of dreams." Finally, we settled on *Chasing the Elusive Dream*. We figured that our fellow Angelenos would recognize how elusive dreams can be in this quirky, competitive, diverse, and unwieldy metropolis.

For this volume, we strove to stay true to the tone and style choices of each writer. This allows us to present an eclectic mix of stories, while giving each writer the freedom to experiment with the short-story medium.

This anthology begins with an otherworldly tale by Sara Chisolm, "The Serenade of the Gangsta." In it, a gangster's future is foretold by a mystical mariachi's song. The dreamy theme continues into "Luigi's Song" by Jude-Marie Green, in which a young girl's best friend is a whale who brings her gifts from the sea.

Summaries don't begin to do these stories justice. These, and those that follow, cover the gamut of love found and lost; life and death; right and wrong; freedom and slavery (and slavery's close cousin, addiction). We present stories of fortunes, both on the rise and in decline.

Nick Duretta's "Lucky and Carmela" takes a chance meeting in an unexpected direction.

"Billboard Cowboy" by Axel Milens features a man in midlife who struggles with his position, both in the world and in his own family.

My own stories cover the Gen X experience, from the nineties until the modern age. A young college student gains assertiveness training from an unexpected source in "College Lessons," while in "Letting Go," a career woman learns to release her ingrained ideas about work, as well as her favorite colleague.

Cody Sisco's "Face" explores L.A.'s underground world of psychic entanglement and seductive illusions.

C. Gregory Thompson's "Two Kings" forces two men from vastly different backgrounds to solve the puzzle that is created when their paths collide.

Nolan Knight's story "Mouth Bay" — a misnomer for the South Bay region because of all the gossip there — showcases the grime beneath the sunshine and glitter.

"For Hire" by A.S. Youngless follows a young werewolf who is pressed to figure out whom she can trust.

James Ferry's "Burning Man" transports readers out of L.A. and into the desert for some soul searching.

Finally, Abigail Walthausen's "Edition of Ten" limits the main character's soul searching to her own neighborhood in L.A. proper.

We hope you will enjoy this new volume of L.A. stories. Some of the writers from the first anthology have returned, while others have joined us for the first time. We're excited to present this new collection, to support our literary community, and to shine some light on more facets of the jewel that is Los Angeles.

— Gabi Lorino

THE SERENADE OF THE GANGSTA

Sara Chisolm

The new Gold Line subway system serves as the backbone of our community, allowing gringos access to Mariachi Plaza. All the good musicians lumber around here with guitars, trumpets, and accordions resting beside them in their cases. Boyle Avenue and First Street box in the oxidized statue of the mother of Ranchera music, Lucha Reyes. The stoic statue has its hands placed on its hips with its back towards a few shops that have colorful murals painted on their sides. Tables and sun-bleached umbrellas line the front of the stores. Lucha's prideful gaze rests on the stone symmetric mirador, the circular pattern of red and white cement ground, an affordable housing complex, and mainly, her fellow musicians: the mariachis.

The mariachis advertise well. Boyle Ave is stitched together with cars, rusty vans, parking ticket-draped hoopties, and even a few lifted trucks emblazoned with logos, phone numbers, and decals of Mother Mary receiving a serenata. Most of the time, black-suited mariachis yell out to subway patrons, soliciting buyers for their band's services. "Who wants a romantic serenade by a live band for their one true love? Or perhaps the person that is just for now?" A few times a week, one of the mariachi singers will belt out a tune, allowing the pedestrians an opportunity to hear a serenata of foretold love and doomed lovers.

When you grow up around here, the serenata is all you hear about. At your family gatherings, you will hear about how so-and-so got engaged and how perfect the serenata had been. Within your school, amongst your friends, someone will bring up how so-and-so is learning to play an instrument so that he can present some girl with a serenata. Or you will hear about how much so-and-so's mariachi band costs for a serenata, so you better save if you want one.

The romantic lures of the serenata never captured my attention. I have always been too busy hustling on the streets to give a damn about romance. I make a lot of money through extorting local businesses and dabbling in drug sales on the sly. My gang is ambitious. We have carved out our territory through savagery. No one is immune to the cruelty of our reign, except the mariachi. They are untouchable.

I've made it no secret among the mariachis that I operate in the select business of "party favors." Everybody knows the true blood of the plaza flows from the lips and fingers of the mariachis. However, you could also say that the blood flows a little easier with the help of the drugs that line my pockets. Manuel, the leader of our gang, is always hesitant about the drug trade. I am different. I am not a pussy. I have a budding rap career. I have to pay for my studio time. I can peddle my goods among the mariachis and not think twice. If a mariachi wants to buy some drugs, then at least it should be from me.

I wasn't surprised when an elderly mariachi dressed all in black velvet approached me. The old man had been standing near the entrance to the metro station where colorful tiles of glass within the metal overhanging canopy looked like broken pieces of stained-glass windows when the sun shined through them. The mosaic of light reflected onto a mounted bust of a woman with upraised hands and a child cradled underneath her.

THE SERENADE OF THE GANGSTA

Now, as he tinkered towards me like some busted wind-up toy, the mariachi's arms waved in the air, giving the illusion that the fingertips of the statue and his own were brushing against one another. The moaning of the lower-level escalator sounded like cries of repentance. His left leg dragged while his guitar case bounced at his side. More than likely he was drunk or high from the last gig's payout. In this area, the promises of Hollywood became no more than a lingered whisper. Where the residents mainly survive on meals of beans and rice, you have to be careful. If he touched me or tried to take my stash of dope, I'd have to put him in his place. Revered or not, if you aren't about this Los Angeles gangsta life, then you better be careful in these streets.

I dug in my pocket. Slipped on some brass knuckles as easily as a new pair of underwear. I propped my hand up on the pocket of my jeans, letting the gleam of the brass greet his arrival.

The usual baby-blue sky and flecks of cruising white clouds were suddenly subdued. The sky was blotched with looming heather overcast. The sun's rays beamed down through gaps in billowy canopy. Cockroaches scurried from every orifice of the plaza, some huge ass ones, skinny ones, and even some with eggsacs bending out of their backsides. My body shivered as if I had felt the sting of my old man's belt. I hated bugs. I shifted my feet and couldn't help but step on some. The crunch of their bodies permeated the slow drawl of the mariachi's throatful hum. I bobbed my head for a second, creating words to his beat in my head. *So many gangstas dreamin' about a rapper's life, I ain't ever given up, I'm get mine, I got a wad of cash so fat you could flatline.* Then the bugs climbed up his legs and disappeared within his black uniform.

3

He smiled, and a feeling of doom washed over me. He was a man that was gray. You could see his teeth were partially transparent. His smile opened up the world; placid steel-colored saliva tainted his mouth. His face was clean-shaven, with patches of flaky eczema that were as dull in color as dry toothpaste on your favorite sweater. He had strands of regal metal-wire hair sticking out from the corners of his tilted black sombrero, embroidered with silver thread.

I blinked a few times and squinted. My eyes searched for the bugs then found them hanging on his suit like decorative buttons. They shined in the absence of the sun.

"Una serenata?" he called out to me.

I took off my baseball cap. My highlighter-bright dreadlocks fell onto my tattooed forehead and eyelids. I flexed the bill of my cap and put it back on. I was not in the mood for the tricks and trade of a drunk.

"Nah man," I barked. I remembered how to say that I didn't want something in Spanish. But long ago, I gave up the polite sing-song words of my home language, replacing it with street slang and thug talk.

"Do you want a serenade?" his melodic voice rung out.

I blinked and shook my head.

"Whatcha want?" I dipped my head low, avoiding his light-grey gaze. I had to make a thousand more dollars if I wanted to pay for a day's worth of studio time. I thought about exit strategies if he attempted to rob me.

He stomped and ground down the heel of his boot, staining the red cement with a splatter of gray bug bits.

I leaned in and said, "You want some weed, pills, trippies … What?"

"Do not worry. I am quite good. Even for the likes of …" He waved his hand up and down my body. "Even for members of the community like you." His Spanish accent drew out. He fumbled with his guitar case. "I can do elderly birthday parties. They usually don't want me for weddings."

I stared hard at him before saying, "Look, old man …"

"Yes, I can see," the mariachi said while nodding, "you are missing the attendance of a good girl's company. Let me put your mind at ease."

"I told you, I am not into that type of shit," I stated. I put my hand on the pocket filled with baggies of drugs. "If you need to party, though …"

The mariachi frowned slightly before explaining, "I am just saying that you are all alone in this world, just as a man is in his own death."

The mariachi lifted a silver-gray guitar out of its dilapidated case. Back in the day, this guitar was beautiful. Now the strings curled up like cat whiskers, but the neck was elegant and sturdy. If I took off with it, I wondered how much money I could've gotten for it. The edges of the instrument's body were blurry, as if you couldn't focus your eyes on them.

"Of course, I do play funerals. I am good there. Sending the dead off to their own personal purgatory."

I hadn't held one since I was a little boy, so I yanked the guitar out of his hands and then held it with affection while I examined it, trying hard to pull the blurry edges of the instrument into focus. I must have been imagining shit. I mentally reminded myself to lay off the weed. Memories of my old man sitting in the living room and strumming his guitarra filled my head whenever I was high, because there are only two things that a man grows up to be if he lives in this neighborhood long enough. You can turn to the streets or pick up an instrument.

"Then perhaps a music lesson or two so that you can become a mariachi?"

I almost laughed in his face, then bit my tongue. "I already told you, old man. I'm a gangsta." I shoved the instrument towards the mariachi.

"You can find redemption in anything," he said.

This time, I laughed and waved my hand by his chest to dismiss him. I turned my back, and he grabbed my arm. "Help an old man out with something to eat?"

I pulled back my fist and swung at him. The brass was my paintbrush as the mariachi's blood decorated the pavement. I saw the glint of the silvery guitar and luminescent shells of the bugs descend to the ground in a clatter. The mariachi's instrument looked more like toy car parts than splinters of wood from a broken guitar. The cockroaches scurried over the splinters and strings, and when they touched the mariachi's broken guitar, they turned into a lucid gray. The old man hunched over his instrument and the bugs scattered, revealing a newer version of the metallic guitar.

The cockroaches climbed over my new Cortez shoes. I kicked at them and stomped, relishing the sound of their exoskeletons succumbing to the weight of my foot. They scattered to the far reaches of the plaza, snatching up all the surrounding color. The bright blue hue of Lucha Reyes's benevolent face, the tan stone of the mirador, and all the buildings in the plaza became a striking, lifeless gray.

"You dropped something," the gray mariachi stated while pointing down.

My inventory of drugs had fallen out of my baggy jeans and onto the concrete. The arrangement of scrunched-up bags of chalky crystals, colorful pills, and green herbs looked like a forbidden garden growing out of the curb. I quickly picked up my stash. I looked around the square at its inhabitants. This was the time when the gangstas on the block targeted the local businesses. With the usual lunch crowd tucked back into work, the businesses were easy, witness-free targets for the picking. We frequented the small wheeled carts, fruit stands, and shops, threatening to put them out of business if they didn't pay up. I saw an associate or two of mine out of the corner of my eye.

A couple of homies walked by; they leaned toward me and gave exaggerated grins. One held out his index and middle finger in my direction, pulled back on the fingers of his other hand, and winked: the universal warning sign of the streets.

"I only wanted to serenade you," the old man bellowed. "So few men are allowed such beauty at a time of devastation and death."

The gray mariachi stood up. As if he had pulled on a string, his hand commanded the neck of the instrument to him. He held the instrument. The old man began to strum his guitar. The instrument vibrated as if it had a pumping heart.

I jumped back out of confusion and fear. I looked around the plaza, checking to see if other people saw what I saw. But the time of the day was all wrong. The middle of the afternoon, when the real gangstas took their gang's cut in the profits of the local businesses, had somehow dissipated to later on in the day.

Midday was in the middle of its natural escape as the sun dipped a little bit lower behind a tower of gray clouds. This was the time when the commuters packed up their backpacks, briefcases, and purses, getting ready to flood the square. Most of the mariachis were setting up for practices, weddings, birthday parties, or the sentimental performances of the surprise serenatas.

I stared at him. His eyes glowed an unearthly sea green. The dullness of his skin was blossoming into a rosy brown tint.

"I wonder what I shall call this one?" He rubbed his chin. "Oh yes. The serenade of the gangsta."

"I — I'm outta here," I stammered.

"It is all the same," he whispered. "The serenata and your death have already begun."

With that said, he began to robustly pluck the guitar strings while he tapped his foot. I ran off, the trail of disgusting cockroaches always a few yards ahead. Their small opaque bodies bleached the neighborhood a monotonous gray.

I ran to the end of the block. The cars whizzed by. The sound of barking dogs could not hide the beauty of the mariachi's voice as it reached my ears.

He didn't sing in English or Spanish but still I understood it. The song soothed me as I rounded another corner to collide with Manuel. My body slammed against the ground. My black baseball cap flipped off. The cheap hair dyes that I had used in the cracked porcelain sink of my mom's house blended to produce a marsh-gray sweat that dripped from my brow.

"This is the end, little brother," the melodic singing of the mariachi stated.

I looked up at Manuel. He was a big guy. The people in our high school said that back in Mexico, Manuel's uncle was a kingpin. When Manuel frowned, his entire face crinkled up like a used brown bag.

"I was just on my way to see you," I laughed nervously.

"Do not fear, little brother," the mariachi sped up his playing as his voice raised in pitch.

Manuel growled. He grabbed me by the collar and lifted me to a standing position. "You know how much I hate it when people arrange their own side deals on my turf. I even heard you punched a mariachi!" Manuel let go of the collar of my shirt, and I greedily choked on air.

Manuel leaned over until the pupils of his eyes clouded my vision. His jacket moved slightly, and I felt him rubbing the barrel of his gray gun against me.

"It won't happen again," I said, my voice quivering. My heart pumped to the fast-paced rhythm of the gray mariachi's guitar. My lips trembled as I gathered the courage to speak. "You know I am working on a mixtape. I am good, Manuel. I can make it out of these streets. I just need a little more. Just a little more. Take it. Take it all." I shoved a stack of bills and bags of drugs into his face.

Some of the bills came loose and fluttered to the sidewalk like empty bubblegum wrappers. My eyes dropped to the green and white money that lay on an unkempt gray lawn. Two hundred bucks. Two hundred dollars was more money than my father ever brought home to us after a serenata.

"You think I just care about the money, *payaso*?" Manuel threw the money and baggies of drugs to the ground. "You really are a clown, huh? When you mess with the mariachi, you lose respect in the community. They turn against you and me."

I looked down at the ground while I shook my head. A gangsta talking about respect? Respect for the mariachis? Manuel wasn't as tough as I had originally thought.

I looked Manuel in the eyes. I couldn't back down now. The streets would ring with word of my cowardice. If you wanted to hustle, you had to sacrifice. I was prepared to do the things that my father never did. Rest my father's tireless soul from the cancer. I was willing to pray to the high heavens for Manuel's bluff. I stuck out my chest. "Do it then. Kill me. Pussy."

"Let's go," he growled.

"Death is like a lover that we sleep next to." The mariachi's voice penetrated the stagnant air.

The community had welcomed the presence of night and its chill too soon. I walked in front of Manuel until we reached an abandoned building, an old drug house boarded up and wrapped in caution tape.

Manuel hit me square in the back with the handle of the gun. "Move," he shouted as I hesitated for a moment.

I walked past the giant weeds that peeked above the overgrown grass on the lawn. The dandelion's ghostly spores looked like comets in the sky as they pulled apart and dispersed as we trampled by. Manuel practically pulled the door off its hinges and pointed the glistening gun into the dark-gray room.

"Death's lingering embrace." The mariachi's voice filled the house up.

We stood in the center of the room. Manuel pointed his gun at my chest. He stepped closer, and I felt a cold circle against my diaphragm. I closed my eyes and flinched in anticipation.

"When death has you, little brother, your fateful lover ..." The mariachi's voice penetrated my clammy skin. I felt the hum of his words as they coursed through me.

The gun was cocked back. I grabbed Manuel's hand and pulled the gun, attempting to tug it from his rough, beefy-handed grip.

"Little brother, kiss your lover, gently hold her close, embrace the death ..." The mariachi's voice kept time with the beating of my heart.

Manuel squeezed the trigger. His body jumped back when the gun fired. I felt the bullet as it ripped through my abdomen.

"Dear little brother," the mariachi's tempo slowed down, "this pain is worse than any broken heart a woman can give you. The way you suffer is the way your last breath escapes you, the way that your skin pales as warmth leaves it, the way that your mother leans across your open casket."

I stepped closer to Manuel. I twisted the gun from his grip. I cocked the gun and fired.

I stared into that bright orb and watched Manuel's pupil shrink down until it was a tiny lifeless mirror of my future. He fell to the ground, taking me with him. I stood up, slipping on blood. I tripped over the steel-gray gun. I sat there, staring at his body for a moment. As a cold sweat began to form over my body, I thought to myself, that is supposed to be me.

For a moment, the world went silent.

I looked down at my white T-shirt, now stained with blood. My shaky hands fiddled with the warm hole in the center of my chest.

A thin layer of dust had already claimed Manuel for the sake of the earth and the life that may spring from it. I reached in my pocket, took out a wad of bills, and placed them at the center of his chest. The money bloomed and brightened in his blood. I folded his stiff graying hands onto his crisp money, a bouquet worthy of his maleficence.

I ran with the low humming of the mariachi's voice in my heart. I ran even more when I felt as if my lungs were about to burst. I ran to the bright man in the black sombrero. When I stumbled into him, I saw that his face had smoothed out to a creaminess that was reminiscent of an avocado. When he smiled at me, his white teeth glistened. He stooped down to put me and his guitarra onto the ground.

"I don't know how you saved me, but you saved me," I panted. The mariachi laughed, and it was as if the whole world shook in joy.

"I told you that that serenata belonged to you, my friend."

"I don't believe in saviors and know very little about redemption, but from this moment on, I pledge to change my life." Sweat was dripping off my chin as the last push of the recent adrenaline rush hijacked my body. I stood up on my shaking legs.

I felt strong and determined to spend this second chance at living a life for the betterment of the community. Maybe I could learn to play the trumpet and be a mariachi, like my old man. I imagined myself in the same black velvet getup as this mariachi.

"Will you teach me? Teach me how to save lives, Mariachi?"

He frowned for a moment, then his face settled into the complacency of contentment.

"Save lives?"

My energy was spent. I licked at my dry lips as I collapsed onto the hard concrete. I stared up at him, enamored. I was dazzled by his charm as he lifted his guitar and pointed his index finger at me while winking.

"Who would say that someone like me saves lives? Taking wayward souls to their rightful place brings life to these old bones of mine."

I blinked up at him, the smell of incense and rot curling into my nostrils. I coughed while inhaling the poignant aroma. Gray cockroaches swarmed the plaza. Like beacons of light, they shined down into every orifice of the square, birthing color back into the world.

"You have to excuse my insect problem. They are just so attracted to the scents of death and the promise of a good meal."

I felt as if I were about to faint. I looked down at my ashen hands.

"You see," the mariachi continued, "you are about to die." The mariachi waved his hands in the air dramatically as the heart-pumping guitar played on its own. "You are seeing the final moments of a life not worthy of living flash before you."

I blinked again, taking note of changes. The pizzeria, the hip bone of our community, reflected the evanescent white glow of the moon from its dark windows. The absence of the gringos who laughed and tilted their plastic champagne cups too high pierced the night. The neatly packed cars were no longer boxing in Boyle Avenue. I had a sensation that without the cars, the very concrete that I sat upon could unravel at any moment, and that we could be floating upon nothingness. Lingering commuters who would be looking at their watches or dispersing into the streets to catch a bus or walk home were nowhere in sight. The most noticeable change was the missing mariachis. The mariachi bands who would have ended their night early and were looking to get lucky with last-minute serenatas had not claimed their spaces on the wrought-iron public benches. The mirador with its tan stone and moderately tilted side was neatly fixed up, looking as foreign to me as a dollhouse. There wasn't even a drunk lingering in sight. The Lucha Reyes statue, with her back turned to the whitewashed walls of the shops, appeared different. Lucha's gaze rested on me. Her face knotted into a scowl of pity or anger as her red rose-petal eyes made contact with mine.

"Where is this place?"

The mariachi strummed his guitar gently as if he were tickling a baby. His melodic tone continued. "Purgatory, Purgatory."

LUIGI'S SONG

Jude-Marie Green

Saturday night in Southern California. On the beach. Near the pier. The famous one you've seen in movies all your life. I'm sitting on this damp mound of sand, perched a few feet above the surf line, waiting for the grunion to bring me a gift. From Luigi. Luigi's a whale.

So what if I'm just about eighteen and don't have a boyfriend? My best friend's a whale. I watch the waves and imagine a night dive, which I can't do as my regular dive partner's busy.

"Alone again, naturally," I almost sing. I never sing. Not even karaoke. Look, my name's Daisy. How's that for lame? I hate it, but I guess I don't have much in the way of imagination cuz I can't think of anything I'd rather be called. You ever see that movie with Barbra Streisand, *On a Clear Day You Can See Forever*? The main character is psychic, talks to plants, has been reincarnated, and sings really corny Broadway numbers, and her name is Daisy, too.

I guess "Daisy" suits me well enough. I don't sing, but that psychic thing? Well, here's the story.

When I'm nine, my 'rents take me to an aquarium. That's like a zoo for fish. A habitrail for humans snakes under some enormous tanks full of swimming and floating creatures. We walk underneath the killer whale exhibit.

I hear them talking to me.

"What is your name?"

15

I hear this, sounding distant and vibraty.

At first I think the 'rents are messing with my head, cuz 'rents like to do stuff like that. Santa Claus, the Easter Bunny, Mr. Ed. Talking whales are not a big leap, if you get my drift. I play along.

"Daisy. What's yours?"

The 'rents jump a little.

Mom says, "What's our what?"

I grin at her and wait for the game to continue.

"We're the whale," that voice says again. I'm staring at my 'rents and their lips don't move, except to form skinny frowns. I'm surprised, but I hold it in pretty well — at least I think I do.

I look up and above me are a couple big black and white bullet-shaped hulks. The nameplate says killer whales. They twirl around and seem to be looking right at me.

I whisper, quiet as I can, "I can't talk right now. Will you be here later?"

Though I guess that's kinda stupid, cuz, where could they go?

Some happy humming, but no words. I'm grinning like a kid with a secret cuz I'm a kid with a secret and a plan.

Now that I'm older, I wonder that I accepted so easy the idea that the fish could talk to me. Or that I could actually understand them, cuz fish talk to everybody, all the time. Noisy little souls. It's just us, we don't hear them. Except me. I hear 'em fine in my head.

The 'rents haul me along through the rest of the displays in the aquarium. We see flat sole, snaky eels, and stringy coral. Now and again I say something like, "How are you today?" but no one answers, at least none of the fish. Once an old lady in a pink hat turns around and says back to me, "I'm fine today, young lady. How are you?"

My 'rents can't believe how sweet I'm being; not that I'm not usually, but usually I'm a lot less outgoing. They worry about that at night when they think I can't hear 'em discussing me. Maybe I should make an effort to be more outgoing all the time. I'm scoring points.

I use the points when we sit down in the fishy-themed restaurant for lunch.

"Can I — I mean, *may* I go to the bathroom please?"

One big hard-and-fast rule of parenting is *Don't let the kids go anywhere alone.* They're afraid of rapists or something, maybe just the evening news. But we're sitting right next to the restrooms. They exchange glances, Mom worried, Dad startled, but they agree in that silent parental way of theirs.

"Okay, go ahead," says Dad.

"Come right back," Mom adds. She watches me until I push open the bathroom door and go through.

As I expect, they aren't watching for me to come back out right away. I wait for an older woman to leave, and I slip out behind her. The 'rents don't see me return to the aquarium.

They find me about an hour later; that is, the security dude finds me. He uses the black walkie-talkie thing on his shoulder to call in the code that I've been found safe and sound, talking to myself.

Of course I'm not talking to myself. I'm chatting with the killer-whale kids.

See, these killer whales grew up here. They aren't whales, by the way; they're kinda like dolphins, and they call themselves The One Tribe. Their mothers told 'em the stories of The One Tribe, about chasing seals and eating penguins and fighting battles with other dolphins. The One Tribe seems violent to me. PG at least. The moms told 'em how they'd rather die than live cut off from the world below, the world of the ocean. So the moms died. But the kids stayed and they like it here.

"Heaven," they call it, this aquarium.

But they're forgetting the stories their moms told 'em and they're happy to tell me: a new audience, right? I promise to come back when I can.

My mom grabs me up in a hug. When she finally lets go, I say, "Mom, don't die."

"What? What do you mean?" She's about to cry, I can tell.

Dad smiles in that fakey parent way and says, "Are you worried we'll leave you alone for running away and scaring us?"

I grab him into a hug, too, and wonder if he can talk himself into dying, like the killer whales' parents did.

And they, the killer whales, the orcas, are happy to be here. I stop talking while the adults buzz around me, crying and thanking and apologizing and everything.

I'm thinking on what the orcas told me.

Show and Tell in school on Monday, and I talk about my trip to the aquarium.

Some kid from the back row says, "My mom says aquariums are bad because the whales are kidnapped from the ocean and put into a prison and 'sploited for our fun." He sticks his tongue out at me, so I have to respond.

"Nuh-uh, the orcas told me they like being in the aquarium. It's clean. And they get lots of food." At least I try to say that. But the kids laugh and the teacher claps her hands to shut them up, and I don't even know what's going on. I look at the teacher and say, "What?"

"Now, Daisy," she says in a super-tolerant voice, "I'm sure that animals did not talk to you. You must mean your parents told you the aquarium is a good place. Whales don't speak."

I see where this is going, so I agree with her and sit down soon as I can. The kids only tease me for a day or two, calling me nuts and inviting me to the loony bin before my mistake is forgotten.

I twig pretty fast that I better not tell anyone else about this, this talent, skill, whatever it is. I never try to share this power of mine, though sometimes it's lonely. Eight years I've kept the secret. But I'm not stupid. No loony bin for me, thank you.

Though I feel pretty silly sitting here on wet sand waiting for the grunion. The night is one like Persian poets would wax lyrical about: scented breezes, crashes of waves, the fat full moon luminous above.

I read *The Rubaiyat of Omar Khayyam* one summer, while waiting for Luigi to return. Those Persians had sand, and I have oceans, but it's the same vast expanse that casual people assume is empty.

I sit here on the sand and wait for the flood of silver bodies. I've done this before, years ago, as a little kid: the midnight run of grunion, tiny fish washed ashore to spawn, laying eggs and spewing sperm before the next wave washes them off to sea again. I remember the creatures thick on the ground, us kids capturing a fleeting few: look Ma, no hooks. Then we'd toss them back into the waves as soon as we were bored. Did I hear them back then? I don't remember. Probably whatever I heard I ignored. Little kids are so accepting.

Tonight I see a few silversides flash, a few dozen perhaps, not the waves of fish that I expect. That I remember.

Grunion are small fish with simple minds. They're thinking about spawning. I sure hate bothering them during sex. Still, they're supposed to have the thing for me.

Luigi's gift. The one he promised me.

So, I talk to them, in Human-speak, which they understand perfectly well even if they don't want to hold a conversation with me right now.

"Do you have it? Where is it? What is it?"

They respond, group voice, annoyed and distracted. For some reason I'm thinking about tiny condoms (hey, I'm a teenager, it's only natural), not about the floating encrusted glass globes that the grunion bring with them and deposit like fist-sized eggs on the wet sand, their little bodies pushing the floats above the surf line.

I step carefully around the silver bodies; no one wants their sex lives disturbed, right? A stack of globes, a bunch, lots. Maybe two dozen. He promised a gift. I only expected one.

The first time I saw one of these floats was the first time I met Luigi. Had to do with a high school project, learning to scuba dive so I could participate in Clean the Ocean Day.

Extra credit, yeah, and a fun way to see the good-looking guys wear swim trunks and show off their buff bods. Of course they looked at me too, I hope. Yeah, I'm pretty sure. I look pretty good in a bikini. But mostly I wanted to get in the water and see if I could still talk to whales.

See, even though I live in SoCal, I'd rather go to the mall than the beach. No one goes in the water. Eww. Every rainy season the news is full of overflowing sewage treatment plants, high bacteria counts, and beach closures. Surfers get this rash caused by the dirty water. The surf foam is yellow and brown, not white and blue-green. I don't want anything to do with that.

But I miss using my "special ability." Everyone has a special ability, right? Mine's talking to whales. I mean, hearing them. But I'm not going to the beach, nuh-uh. And the killer whales at the aquarium bore me; I got sick of their constant happy blathering years ago. But down in the ocean, if I could check out the whales in the ocean, I'm sure I'd hear something new.

So anyway. Scuba. The 'rents won't let me learn when I'm a kid 'cause they say it's a dangerous hobby. All that stuff about nitrogen narcosis and depth gauges and air pressure. It's expensive too, but I don't think the 'rents care about that. Still, till I'm sixteen, I can't do it without their permission, and I can't get their permission. Instead, they take me whale watching.

Whale watching season in SoCal is February through April. Half-off the ticket price if you don't see any whales, but we always see some. I'm never close enough to talk to the creatures, but I hear what they sing. They are happy. Gloriously free and happy, especially when they breach: jump outta the water into the air and fly into heaven.

That's what their songs say. "Heaven."

Now, these aren't aquarium whales performing circus acts for bits of cut-up fish. These are California gray whales — huge creatures, thirty feet long, covered in barnacles and riddled with scars.

I'm in love.

I want to talk to them. So, when the opportunity comes up to learn scuba through school, and I'm sixteen, and the 'rents can't raise enough objections, I sign up for the class.

The instructors are a little dopey. What can you expect from people who live in the water all the time? The instructor in charge was once a Navy SEAL. Of course I know what that is. I watch the movies. He's a little pudgy, old, and still has the shaved head like in his Navy SEAL photos, which are tacked all over the walls in his office. The other instructors, a beach-bunny type girl with a tan and a guy with dreads, also strike me as bubbly playacting types, beach types, not serious.

They're dead serious about the training and equipment, though.

After the class gets certified, we do the Clean the Ocean thing. OMG. I don't see much in the way of fish, but plenty of garbage floating in the water, on the sandy bottom, and entangled in the seaweed stuff growing everywhere. Plastic, mostly, but other stuff too. Soggy cigarette boxes. Broken beer bottles. I grab as much of the crap as I can and stick it into my net sack. I have thirty minutes of air, but I fill the sack in ten minutes.

So, I get the extra credit and a close-up view of the ocean bottom.

How can I describe the bottom? It's green. Everything is green or gray, except some of the fish. And the trash. Sunlight flashes through the water, refracting off suspended particles and sparkling down on us like dust motes dancing in a partially lit, shadow-filled room. Like that, but wet.

And it's full of fish. Don't chase the fish. Don't touch the fish, either. But sometimes they'll come up and nibble on my fingers, the bare parts of my legs, and my cheeks. Feels like the most fabulously delicate kisses.

I hang out at the dive office so much, looking for a dive partner, that Dreads starts going out with me most weekends. He's not my boyfriend, don't even think it. He and Sedna, the girl I thought was a beach bunny but is actually kinda cool, they have a thing going.

But I like to dive all the time, and Sedna works, and Dreads (okay, his name is Charlie, but I call him Dreads and he likes it) has the time.

Round about December, Dreads says, "The gray whales are migrating. Let's go out and see them."

I love this idea.

Dreads almost backs out, he was busy he said, but I whine until he gives in. "All right, no problem, geez. I've never known anyone so intense about diving."

Hey. That is a pretty cool compliment, isn't it?

So, we're in the water, we're dive partners and aren't too far from each other ever. Still I'm surprised when he grabs my shoulder and points. I follow where he's pointing and yeah, there they are.

Gray whales. Enormous humpy creatures, barnacles on their skin and small fish darting around them. I laugh. They are beautiful.

Dreads is trying to pull me up, away, but I make a slashing motion with my hand, diver speak for "no, not yet."

Not yet. The whales are talking.

My tank is near exhausted, a good five minutes past what I should have used, when I decide to go up. Dreads is near hysterics and wants to skip the safety stop, dangerous, but I'm not worried; I'm almost giddy.

The whales tell stories to each other. And me cuz I'm listening in. I hear part of an epic poem about migrating to the other great ocean. A couple start a call-and-response song about courtship so blunt that I'd blush except it's so sweet. Someone sings a quiet song comparing the perfect water long ago to the hard-to-tolerate water nowadays. The others shush him, ignore him.

I'm ashamed. But I'm also curious.

Are they so different from me, these creatures? Aside from being huge and ocean dwelling?

I climb on board and shed my gear. Dreads is ready to yell at me, but I say, "Hush, they're breaching over there."

The whole pod, maybe six creatures, dance around the boat. They sing happy.

I yell back at them, "You're beautiful!"

23

They sing, "We're beautiful!"

I yell, "You're beautiful!"

One particular whale swims close to the boat and snorts up at me.

"Come swim with us," he says in Whale.

"Okay," I say in Human. "I'll be right down."

I take about five minutes to pull on my fresh tanks, rebreather, mask, and I take the giant step. Dreads is a few moments behind me, grousing about crazy women, and he's upset that I jump before he's ready. Always take a partner, right? But the whale will be my partner.

I'm bobbing in the water and the creature is startled that I'm in there with him and skims away, but he floats back again soon.

"Swim with me," he says.

"That's what I'm doing," I say. The whale flails, then speaks to me again.

"You understand me?"

"Well, duh," I say. "I'm speaking to you, aren't I?"

And so that's how I meet Luigi. That's as close as I can get to pronouncing his name. Also, I kinda like the idea of a pizza-making whale.

We talk for a while, exchanging stories. He says whales don't avoid people as much anymore cuz people don't kill them so much anymore. He says he can sing the names of his family killed by people. He says people took the bodies but couldn't take the songs.

He sounds kinda angry when he says this, so I say in a big hurry, "Yeah, I bet the spirits all go to heaven, huh?"

And so he asks me about heaven.

And he asks where bad spirits go.

I tell him about hell. What I know of it, anyway. Fire and brimstone — which is only sulfur, after all — and eternal torment.

"So, heaven's the sky? And hell is beneath the bottom?" Luigi considers this for a moment, then says, "I've lived between heaven and hell all my life! I live in the ocean!"

We both laugh a little. I tell him that heaven and hell are ideas, not real places.

He thinks about all this, his big eyes rolling at me. He says there is no heaven or hell for his family; there's just being alive and being remembered.

My tank alarm goes off, and I realize I have to leave; only have thirty minutes of air, right? And only two dives today, I can't do more. As I make my way back up to the boat, Luigi tells me that his pod is finding the warmth south of here. He says they'll be back in four months. He says he hopes to see me again.

He gives me something, an irregular-shaped bit of stone that he coughs up out of his mouth. Eww. Bigger than my fist. I stick it in my net bag and swim slowly away.

I don't tell Dreads that a whale gave me a gift. Who'd believe it? Remember, I'm trying to stay out of the loony bin.

When I get home, I put the stone, a roly-poly bumpy thing of yellow glass, white sand, red shells and all colors of plastic, on my bookshelf. I figure it'll be safe there.

It sure looks like a float, one of those glass balls that fishermen put under their nets. I think for a while on where the float came from and figure if the whale made it, there's only one way. Glass needs heat, right? Sometimes when an earthquake hits, a fissure opens in the ocean floor. Not the end of the world or anything, just some magma flowing into the water.

That must be where he made this float.

Just so's you know, earthquakes are a California given. No place on Earth is immune to seismic activity, I read that in some geology book, but somehow only us

Californians accept the shaking with a smile. What's the big deal? Not like you can predict one beforehand or avoid it during. Grin and bear it, that's my motto.

I didn't know the float was hollow. I suppose a scientist would have figured it out somehow, but I felt the weight of mine and assumed solidness. Maybe if it had sloshed or something, but nope. I found out my float was hollow during an earthquake.

Four in the morning is a rotten time to wake up, especially if the bed is swaying and the ground is moaning and the dumb cat is running around like he's on fire and the bookcase is tilting over.

I know better than to try and stop a falling piece of furniture.

The books plop out, cascading onto the floor. My trophies fall over and land on the books. The float slides off the shelf and shatters.

Mind you, the earthquake itself only lasts a few seconds. The bookshelf falls for longer than that. The house is in utter silence. I hear the words with utter clarity.

It's music, a song. It takes a moment for me to understand I'm hearing words, English, Human-speak. I don't have a head for lyrics and don't have time to write the words down, but I remember. They're sad. The tune is sad, the words mournful.

My 'rents are waking up and moving around and yell from across the house asking if I'm okay. Of course I am. But I'm confused.

I gather up the bits of float; it broke into thick chunks, maybe five pieces. The glassy bits outside are brilliant yellow, sun yellow, daffodil yellow. The insides are mother-of-pearl cream colored, iridescent if you look at it just right. I stroke the inside surface, thinking maybe I'd hear the words again, but no. Nothing but the smooth, soft insides.

You can bet that I have Dreads on the water for the entire rest of whale watching season. I talk with every pod I see passing, tell them my name, ask after Luigi. I see maybe a hundred whales that season. None of them want to converse with me, but they all talk. And sing. And I get another couple floats.

They use the trash we humans throw at 'em, our manna into their desert — empty Coke bottles and plastic grocery bags and pantyhose and diapers — and somehow transform them into the shining shell-encrusted floats, using fire and water and I don't know what kind of tools, or maybe just their flippers and fins.

Somehow they get their songs inside. Their prayers.

Towards the end of whale watching season, in late March, I see Luigi again. This time he's headed north.

Luigi says he's sick. He wants to go to heaven, he says.

I've long since gotten past all the mythologies my 'rents told me (I like that word better than "lies," don't you?), and I know all this praying won't do a damned thing for Luigi, but I like this church, St. Francis by the Sea, all stained-glass windows and copper ceiling ribs greened by the ocean mist. The quiet in here almost quiets my insides.

I pray to St. Francis to help my friend Luigi. I even put some coins in the collection plate and light a candle — one of the yellow votives, cuz Luigi likes yellow.

Hard to wait through another year for another whale watching season, so I find out as much about whales as I can, and I read poetry, and I learn some stuff about making glass. I figure I could sell these whale floats for a fortune, if I could convince a dealer that they were made by whales. Once again, though, I'd prefer to remain unmedicated.

I do smash open one more float. The words are some-one's story. The voice is not Luigi's; it's different, and sad, and young.

I can't figure out how they're getting voices into the floats, and it's making me crazy. Some kind of tool? Imagining a whale using a recording device — talking into a microphone — is even weirder than imagining them making the globes in the first place.

Of course there's always magic. Luigi in a wizard's hat and tapping a float with a magic wand while chanting a spell. Well, geez. Come on.

And then there's the possibility I'm imagining it. Maybe the voices aren't real. Maybe they never have been.

But they sound real to me.

I see Luigi at the beginning of November, and he doesn't want to play. He says he's tired; he wants to speak with me again when he returns from the warmth during March's full moon. He says he has a gift for me.

Other pods, other whales, pass the word. Wait on the night of the full moon, wait for the grunion, wait for the gift. I tell myself I'm imagining sadness in the songs, melancholy when they say Luigi's name.

Now I have the grunion gifts piled at my feet. Some are yellow — Luigi's artwork — but I see many colors embedded in the floats. So many. Why so many?

I don't know if I've mentioned that I can't understand all the creatures from the sea. For some reason, dolphins and I don't communicate well, but there's a dolphin breaching the night surf a few feet away from me, and he's not swimming away. He doesn't articulate well, but he manages to get his message across.

He sings, "Luigi" — or something that sounds like Luigi's name — "is near, going to heaven, going to heaven, going now." The dolphin ducks under the waves then comes back up. "Going now, going now, going." The dolphin ducks under and stays away.

California gray whales are big. I shouldn't have any trouble seeing him under this brilliant moonlight, even though it's way late at night. Early morning, even. I look north along the beach and nothing. I look south and see spume. I toss the globes into my net bag and run.

The waves crash in and slide out, crash in and slide out, crash in and bring Luigi with them. He surges onto the beach with help from the tide.

I scream. "No! Luigi! No! No, go back, go back, you can't."

But he can. And he does.

I sink to my knees beside him. He's huge, of course, but somehow he looks smaller here, shrunken somehow, than he ever looked under water. I rub my hand across his flukes, and I know he can feel me. He speaks very quietly.

Some tribe or another of American Indians would chant a song before they died, if they knew they were about to die or if they were going into a fierce battle, and the song would be all about their lives and happiness and desires. Their autobiographies, with feelings.

That's what Luigi tells me between the stanzas about his pod and his friends. How he loves to swim with certain fish and hates the smell of others. He says the same chorus over and over again. After the second time I join in.

"I live between heaven above and hell below."

I sing it in his language, and he doesn't correct my pronunciation. Tears flow from my cheeks onto his skin, but he probably can't feel them. Hot salt water isn't much different from cold salt water, right? At least I hope he can't. His song is mostly happy.

Whale rescue shows up, a half-dozen people from a network that phones them when a whale beaches. They try to push me away from Luigi, but I'm not going anywhere. Every time I lose contact with his skin he flails and they back away. After a few times, they leave me be. But they still try to push Luigi into the water. They work at it for hours, and I have to admire their energy.

He's not going.

Luigi is breathing hard, trying to sing his last song. I hear his lyrics — he's a master poet, and I want to sing with him, but I can't form his words correctly. I get the sense, though.

Heaven isn't what he expected. The weight of the world pressing down on him, the cold eyes of humans.

I'm such a failure. I feel that failure like gravity feels to Luigi.

"I can't help you," I say to him in English. In Human-speak.

He knows. He breathes something that sounds like forgiveness.

With the sun, the inevitable news van pulls up. Some pretty woman in a tan polyester suit and high heels staggers across the sand to Luigi. A skinny guy with a professional-grade video camera follows her. He points his camera at us when Luigi coughs up his last breath, delivers one last float to me. Dies.

The reporter is here to talk to the rescuers about the dead, pretending to care about Luigi; that'll last until her next assignment. She begins to poke the microphone in my face, but I turn away. I look pretty dramatic, I bet, with all the tears on my face. I hate this.

And I have a better idea.

I select a green globe from the pile at my feet. I wind up my pitching arm: good hard underhand pitch. The impact rocks that van and scars the white paint job. Even from this far away I can hear the message released from the globe.

I throw another.

Another.

"Listen to that, you bastards!" I'm screaming. Tears and snot and sweat, all in the open on my face. "Listen to that!"

The woman stands shocked and slack-jawed, but the guy with the camera is watching. He's got the camera on his shoulder, switching from focus on me to follow the pitch and focus on the van where the float explodes.

The camera jerks on his shoulder when he realizes what he's hearing. I grab a yellow globe; one of Luigi's. My pitching arm aches now, but I cock it back as well as I can.

"That's for Luigi!"

The camera guy nods. He records the whole thing.

I fall to my knees on the soft hot sand, the clean combed sand, next to the few remaining floats. I can wait to hear these messages.

For now, I'm just glad that someone else is gonna hear Luigi's songs.

LUCKY AND CARMELA

Nick Duretta

Lucky checked the delivery order again. 5602 Woodlawn Street. He looked around. The GPS had directed him to a side street two blocks from an abandoned foundry in East L.A. It was a stretch of asphalt with potholes and weeds growing between cracks, lined with time-worn prewar homes — windows barred, fronted by parched, debris-strewn lawns riddled with weeds, some surrounded by prison-like gates. A few cars sat in driveways or on the street, their paint dulled by the constant sun, chrome plagued by rust, tires bald.

He pulled up to 5602, one of the more presentable homes on the street. Its blue stucco façade was mostly free of pits and scars, and the few small shrubs in the yard looked healthy and cared for. Still, it didn't look like the house of someone who would be receiving, as a gift, a new hyper-orange BMW Z4 sDrive35is with light alloy double-spoke wheels.

Lucky texted the dealership again to confirm the address, which they did, as well as the name on the order: Davina Morse. Okay then. This must be the place. He brought the transport truck to a stop before the vacant driveway.

Stepping out of the cab, Lucky felt vulnerable. The neighborhoods to which he normally made deliveries were in secure, often gated communities. This one was different, to say the least.

He looked at the address again and walked up to the front door. A small lightstrip spelling *Feliz Navidad* hung on the wall beside it, even though it was May. A Univision *telenovela* blared from a television inside, so someone was home. There was no doorbell. Lucky opened the screen and rapped on the door. After a few moments with no response he rapped again, more strongly.

A pretty, young, dark-haired woman opened the door, cradling a baby in one arm.

"Who are you?" she asked Lucky suspiciously. Then she looked beyond him to the bright orange car sitting on the truckbed, with the oversized red bow on top. "What the fuck is that?"

"Are you ..." Lucky checked the order in his hand again. "Are you Davina Morse?"

The woman blurted out a laugh. "Hell no. I'm Carmela. Carmela Sanchez."

"Is there a Davina Morse at this address?" he asked, even though he already knew the answer.

Transferring the baby, who'd been observing all of this in wide-eyed wonder, to her other arm, Carmela said, "Okay, this some kind of joke, right? What, like somebody would buy me a high-class car like that one out there? What is it, a Mercedes?"

"No, a BMW," Lucky responded. He knew he should make apologies and head back to the dealership. But he liked Carmela's face, fresh and smooth. Her brown eyes shone like polished stones.

He briefly explained that the address on the delivery order matched hers, but the name didn't. She smiled and said that gave her some rights. She asked him if she could take the car for a drive. "Yeah, I know I'm not that Davina lady, but it's my address, right?"

"I can't do something like that," Lucky protested. "I'd lose my job." Even as he said the words, he knew he'd let her do what she asked. He liked her smile. When she cocked her head and acted offended, that clinched it. Okay, just a drive around the block. Even that was wrong but he'd let her do it.

She quickly ran off to deposit the baby with a neighbor ("It's my sister's kid, she won't mind.") She watched Lucky lower the ramp of the truck and back the bow-bedecked car down to the street. He got out, and she climbed into the driver's seat, pulling the seat belt around her.

"You got a license?" Lucky asked after he got into the passenger seat.

"Course I got a license," Carmela replied. "Gimme the key."

He began to hand it to her, and when he hesitated she grabbed the key and fired up the engine, enjoying the sound. She looked with amazement at the controls. "Man, I never drove a car like this one!"

Lucky smiled. "It's six cylinders with two mono-scroll turbochargers. Three hundred thirty-five horsepower. Direct fuel injection."

"Don't know what all that means, but man, is this thing cool." She gunned the engine again, moved the gear-shift into drive, and swung out into the street in a fast swoop. Lucky was impressed by her self-assurance.

"What's your name, anyway?" she asked.

"Lucky," he replied, wondering if he should tell her to slow down. Would the dealer's insurance cover this?

"Lucky? That really your name?"

"Course not. It's Lucero. But they call me Lucky."

She let out a hoot of a laugh. "Well, you sure are lucky for me today. Where do you wanna go?"

"We can't go far," Lucky said. Why the hell did he agree to this? "I don't have time. I gotta take this to the right person."

"How is she gonna know?" Carmela said, turning right at the corner. "Let's go down here. I know some people. They'll freak when they see me driving this."

She slowed in front of a house where three women were sitting on plastic chairs in the front yard, smoking and drinking from cans of beer. Kids splashed in a small rubber pool. Carmela stopped and sounded the car's horn. The women looked up, wide-eyed, and ran out to the car.

"Fuck, Carmela! You win the lotto?"

"Check you out, girl!"

"*Es tuya, guapa?*"

Carmela beamed. "It's my birthday present!"

"It ain't your birthday, *mentirosa*!"

"That your boyfriend?"

Lucky could only think of how many rules he was breaking. He put his hand on Carmela's arm. "We gotta go," he said.

"This is Lucky," Carmela said to the women. "He's taking me to Vegas." Before her friends could respond, she peeled off, the tires screeching.

"Hey, cool it!" Lucky warned.

Carmela let loose another laugh and slowed. "Just want to show off a little, okay? When I get a chance to do that?"

Lucky noticed that, rather than drive toward her house, Carmela turned onto a busier street, the boulevard that connected with the freeway. "So, what about it?" she asked. "Let's go to Vegas. Let's go to the desert."

"You kidding?" he said. What was happening to him? "That would take hours. I'd lose my job for sure."

"What, you got such a special job, delivering cars? You never want to do something crazy?"

She flashed him a wicked smile. Lucky liked the way her smile formed small dimples. He liked her clean scent, and the way her T-shirt fit her tight in all the right places. He pictured himself and Carmela tearing the bow off the top of the car and pushing the Z4 to its limits on the I-15.

"You bring out the devil in me, you know that?" he said with a smile of his own.

She reached over and squeezed his neck. "Then let's do it! We don't need to pack toothbrushes or nothing. Just for a day. What do you say?"

Lucky saw the wild spirit behind Carmela's eyes, in her smile. He felt like he was in a dream, cruising down the street in a fine car with a pretty girl. It had been a long time since a girl this fine had smiled at him that way, not since that sexy bridesmaid at his brother Tomas' wedding the previous year. Of course, he was no fool. He knew that the Z4 had something to do with Carmela's interest. But she had a way of making him feel as special as the car.

"Okay," he said, and watched her face light up even more. "I'll go to Vegas with you."

She pulled over to the side of the street, stopped the car, leaned over and kissed Lucky on the lips. "Now you're talkin'!"

"But," he said, "we can't take this car. I know the delivery order had your address on it and all, but this car don't belong to you, and it don't belong to me. We'd be stealing. I wouldn't just lose my job. I could go to jail."

Carmela's smile deflated, replaced by a disappointed pout.

"But I got a car," he said. "It ain't no Z4, but it's nice, a 750, not too old."

She looked at him and a trace of smile returned. "That a BMW too?"

Lucky nodded. Carmela grinned, kissed him again — less enthusiastically than before, but with more feeling — and pulled back onto the street. At the next intersection she turned left, and then left again, heading back to her house on Woodlawn Street.

Lucky's cell phone chimed as Carmela pulled up behind the transport truck. "Yeah?" he said as he held it to his ear. A few moments later he said, "Sure, I can make it there today. There's still time. But I need to ask something. I'd like to take tomorrow off. Sort of an emergency. That be okay?" He smiled and put the phone back in his pocket.

"They got the address wrong," he said to Carmela.

"Well, no shit."

"It's five-one-six-zero-two. They left out the one. It's on another Woodlawn Street, on the other side of town."

They sat in silence for a few moments.

"Hope you're not too disappointed," he said.

Carmela turned toward him and flashed him that smile with those half-dimples. The afternoon sun bathed her face in a brilliant light. Lucky had never seen anything so beautiful. "Disappointed?" she asked. "Who's disappointed?"

BILLBOARD COWBOY

Axel Milens

Even after all these years, I still wake up drenched in sweat. The nightmares take me back to that afternoon in 1994. The old guilt swells up, fresh and raw, and I have to ask again: *Was it my fault?*

I was twelve at the time. We had driven over the hills to North Hollywood and were parked in front of my cousins' house, a one-story stucco box with windows secured by rusty metal bars. I sat in the back seat of our Pontiac Grand Prix without moving, holding the handle of the open door while my mother sighed with annoyance.

"I'll pick you up after my dentist appointment," she said. "Get out."

"Don't leave me here," I whined. But I had already admitted defeat and stepped out of the car under her impatient glare. I slammed the door, and she took off in a haze of blue smoke.

I stood alone on the pavement, my lungs filling up with Valley smog, the hum of the 101 Freeway behind me, half a block away. I looked at the yard full of dry weeds and at the headless garden gnome lying against the wall. Except for Stephanie, my beautiful fourteen-year-old cousin, I didn't care much for anyone in that house.

I kicked my way up the concrete path oddly lined with pink and lavender river rocks, most likely another of my cousin Charles's art projects. I pressed the doorbell and waited. Next door, old cars and trucks were parked over a dead lawn. Appetizing whiffs of carne asada and voices of men talking in Spanish floated through the air.

With a brusque swish, the front door opened, startling me. Aunt Paulette, a six-foot-tall bag of bones, as my mother called her, filled the doorframe, looking down at me.

"It's me. Bobby," I said, unsure she recognized me as I could not see past her wrap-around sunglasses. She had only one eye, having lost the other — and her right forearm — in a motorcycle accident. She'd been riding behind my uncle, somewhere on the Riviera where he was filming a movie, and they'd smashed into a truck. He'd married her and brought her back to Los Angeles.

"I'm not blind, you know," she snapped with a heavy French accent, pinching her glossy red lips. Her curly brown hair looked like a well-trimmed bush around her head. She wore a flowery silk blouse, a tight knee-length black skirt and high heels. I was expecting an invitation to enter, but, instead, her eyes on me, she raised her prosthetic arm and took a drag from a cigarette stuck between two stiff plastic fingers. The fake flesh-colored hand, freakishly realistic, went back down slowly as jets of smoke shot out of her nostrils.

"Baby!" my aunt called impatiently, turning her head to the side. Charles, my cousin, a chubby twelve-year-old with the dirty shadow of a mustache on his upper lip, was still referred to as "Baby" by my aunt and his sisters, something I laughed about with my mother. Then, a trail of smoke floating behind her, she marched away, heels clacking on the linoleum floor.

I entered and, as I closed the door, I was smacked by a stench of cold tobacco and stale cooking odors. Blowing air out of my nose, trying not to inhale until I got used to the smell, I walked along the dark corridor towards the voices coming out of Stephanie's bedroom.

I peeked inside. Charles was sitting in front of a mirrored dresser while Marie-Ange, my oldest cousin, a sixteen-year-old replica of her mother, wrapped a red towel over his shoulders. Stephanie, in a pink Little Mermaid T-shirt and washed-out jean shorts, sat on the bed, arms hanging over the edge, watching her brother and sister.

Charles caught my eyes in the mirror's reflection. "Hey, it's Tinkle Bell!" he said in a high-pitched voice. He never missed an opportunity to bring up the embarrassing bedwetting accident that had happened years ago during a sleepover. I blushed as the girls turned towards me at the same time and burst out laughing. Charles sang, "Tinkle, Tinkle, Little Star," his double-chin swaying from side to side, then, satisfied, cackled like the big turkey that he was.

"Shut up!" I said. Six months ago, I could've wrestled him to the ground and pushed his fat face into the dirty carpet, but now it was impossible. He'd started to grow and was taller than me by a head and heavier by at least twenty-five pounds. I waited, stone-faced, for the laughter to stop, forgiving Stephanie because hers sounded like the fresh trickle of a fountain and always delighted me.

"Our project for today," announced Marie-Ange with the authority of a schoolteacher, "is to turn Charles into a girl." She leaned back and squinted at her brother like an artist assessing a model as her hand foraged slowly in a purse full of make-up utensils. Charles, staring at himself in the mirror with raised eyebrows, cocked his head to the side and pouted.

"Into a slutty girl," he said.

The girls giggled, and I smiled uncomfortably. "When did your hair start turning blond?" I asked.

"It's bleached tips, dummy," said Charles, rolling his eyes. "Where have you been? Under a rock?"

I opened my mouth, trying to come up with a smart comeback but couldn't.

"Make sure you don't get make-up on my new scarf, Angie," Charles whined as his sister applied some sort of cream on his forehead with a pad. Jerking his chin up left and then right, he pushed down the purple silk handkerchief tied around his neck underneath the collar of his yellow polo shirt and adjusted the red towel over it.

"Jeez, stop moving!" said Marie-Ange. She pressed the pad harder against his face and Charles gave a plaintive yelp.

Stephanie had spread out on the bed, and her long slim legs stretched over the bedspread. With a dreamy gaze, she watched her brother and sister, head resting on one hand over her bent elbow. She never said or did much. Her blonde bangs, which usually swayed like a curtain in the breeze when she walked, hung sideways. Unlike Marie-Ange and Charles, who resembled Aunt Paulette, she had inherited the all-American good looks of her father.

I sat down on the bed with hesitation. At that same moment, she moved her leg up and her calf rubbed against my lower back, lifting my T-shirt. I felt the warmth of her skin against mine, and my heart jumped. I wondered if she had done it intentionally and glanced at her, but she was just watching the make-up session. Disappointed, I looked at her nipples perking up under her shirt. I wondered how it would feel to hold one of her small breasts in the cup of my hand.

"Stephie, Bobby is looking at your titties!" squealed Charles, who had been observing me in the mirror.

"Bobby!" yelled Stephanie. She rolled on the bed and covered her breasts with both hands and fixed her big blue eyes on me.

"I was not," I said, feeling my face burn.

"I bet he wants to suck on them like a little baby," said Marie-Ange without interrupting her work.

"You want some milk from mummy's boobies, baby-boy?" added Charles in a childish voice. The three of them burst out laughing again, Stephanie, her hands still on her breasts, sounding louder and snarkier than the others.

This time, I didn't appreciate the tone of her laugh. I felt tears coming to my eyes, and I stamped out of the room.

In the corridor, I paused and hit the wall silently with my fists, biting my lip until it hurt. My mother would never force me again to visit my cousins, I decided. Feeling better, I made my way toward the living room, peeking through the open door of the kitchen. Aunt Paulette, a cigarette dangling from her pinched lips, was pulling a cookie sheet out of the oven with a battered gray mitt, her artificial arm high up in the air. I wondered how fast it would melt if she stuck it in the oven, and I pictured the melted plastic looking like the old pink bubble gum stuck underneath my school desk.

As always, my Uncle Larry was slouched in a sagging brown armchair, his hairy bare feet with cracked yellow nails framing the TV set. The basketball game was on.

"How the Lakers doing?" I asked, overly enthusiastic. Whenever I saw him, I always felt the need to be cheery and uplifting.

"Hey, little man," he answered with a dull, tired voice. He lifted his closed fist without moving the rest of his body, keeping his eyes on the screen. We bumped fists softly, and his forearm fell back on the armrest with a thump. His stomach stuck out in a round paunch, stretching his white T-shirt.

"Van Exel's doing good," he said, his voice trailing off.

I looked down at the grayish skin of his skull, visible through his thinning blond hair. It was hard to believe Uncle Larry had been a successful actor in the seventies, playing the loud-mouthed tough guy in several movies. Later, for a while, he'd impersonated a rugged cowboy for a brand of cigarettes and his chiseled face had been plastered on billboards all over the country. As of late, he was the night manager of a Blockbuster video store.

"What about Divac?" I asked to revive the conversation. When I was much younger, he used to grab me by the wrists and spin me around until I screamed, then slap his thighs and laugh very loud, his white teeth glistening inside his mouth. Now, he reminded me of a sad old dog waiting to die. I wished he'd pick himself up and become his old self again.

"Divac's working it," he mumbled. "Not at his best, today."

We watched the game for a while, listening to Chick Hearn's grating voice. I was standing next to Larry, touching the worn fabric of his armchair, which felt like the fur of my old teddy bear. Through the sliding glass doors of the living room, I could see the massive pine tree looming over the entire backyard. Underneath, a thick layer of brown pine needles covered the ground. From a branch, a broken swing hung by one rope. On the left, behind the low chain-link fence that enclosed the yard, a group of men poured beer from a keg and drank from red plastic cups while thick gray smoke swirled up into the air from a barbeque. One of them wore a blue cap.

The music on the TV became louder as a Chevy truck bounced down a muddy mountain trail on the screen.

"Are we gonna go shooting?" I asked in a low voice, leaning over. The last time I was here, my uncle had placed his index finger on his lips and gestured to follow him into the garage. After closing the door carefully, he'd unlocked the trunk of his battered Toyota Corolla.

"Check this out," he said, with a hint of pride. A long object was lying inside, wrapped in a plaid blanket, which he ceremoniously flipped to reveal a brand-new shotgun. "Mossberg 500, twelve-gauge pump action."

"Can I hold it?" I asked, mesmerized by the gleaming blue steel of the barrel. He lifted the weapon delicately and presented it to me like a precious object. With excitement, I felt the shotgun's satisfying weight, the hardness of the fore grip in my left hand and the cold metal of the trigger under my index finger. I brought it up to my cheek, placed the butt in the pocket of my shoulder, then aimed the muzzle at a pile of cardboard boxes stacked against the wall. "Bam! Bam!" I said, pretending to shoot, shucking the fore grip back and forth a few times.

"Okay, that's good," said my uncle, taking the shotgun away and putting it back in the trunk. "Our little secret, right Bobby?" he said somberly as he wrapped it tightly.

"What did you get it for?" I asked, wondering why all the mystery.

Uncle Larry hesitated. His head blocked the light and his face was in the shadow. "You never know," he whispered after a moment. Then he seemed to switch back to fun old Uncle Larry for a second and enthusiastically added, "Maybe you and I could go to the gun range and try it out? What do you say?"

The basketball game was back on.

"So, are we going shooting?" I asked again.

My uncle waved his hand, as if chasing a fly.

"One of these days, soon."

45

"Can I see it again?"

"It's locked up. Out there," he said, pointing towards the back of the garden, at a small wooden shed painted green, which I remembered was full of rusty tools.

Suddenly, from the kitchen, Aunt Paulette's high-pitched laugh erupted, immediately followed by the gleeful howling of my cousins. "Oh, Baby!" she squealed, "You're such a pretty girl!" The excitement among the four of them crescendoed as she kept repeating, "Such a pretty girl," in between bursts of laughter while Uncle Larry stared at the TV, a blank expression on his slackened face.

Finally, the ruckus subsided and, after one last snort, my aunt commanded, "Girls, it's time for tea." Soon, my cousins barged in. Marie-Ange was first, with a white table-cloth under her arm that she unfolded in one swift gesture over the dining room table, set right behind the sofa about ten feet from the TV. Stephanie followed, carrying a tray of cups, saucers, spoons, and a sugar bowl against her belly. Charles was last, holding a plate of cookies with both hands.

"Hello, Papa!" he yelled out as soon as he came in, addressing his father from behind the sofa. "How is the game, Papa?"

I stared at Charles in awe. His lips were painted bright red. His fake eyelashes were thick with mascara, his eyelids coated with electric-blue eye shadow. His chubby cheeks had a pinkish glow and a purple elastic hairband encircled his forehead, holding back his hair in a wreath. He wore what looked like one of his mother's bright flower-patterned dresses, cinched at the waist by a large yellow belt. On his feet were pink furry slippers with heels. He reminded me of someone, but I couldn't figure out who.

I stepped back and looked at my uncle to see his reaction. Marie-Ange, a sly smile at the corner of her mouth, and Stephanie, clutching her hands, were doing the same.

Without a word, without looking at anyone, my uncle calmly stood up, walked to the sliding door, opened it, and stepped out. There was a soft hissing sound and a discreet snap as he closed it behind him. We watched him walk away towards the pine tree as Divac scored a buzzer beater and the mad cheers of the crowd rose from the TV.

"Tinkle, Tinkle, Little Star," sang Charles sadly, but this time, to my relief, nobody laughed. He dropped the plate of cookies on the table as Aunt Paulette was entering with a steaming teapot. Eyes to the floor, he turned towards his mother. "He didn't look at me," he said softly, his voice breaking at the end of the sentence.

She stopped, holding the teapot up in the air.

"He wouldn't even look at me," said Charles with a higher pitch, shaking in place with his eyes closed, breathing in and out rapidly.

My aunt's face turned white. "Where is he?" she asked, glaring at the empty armchair.

"He just went outside," I blurted, trying to imply Uncle Larry had done nothing wrong.

The dark glasses glowered silently at me for what seemed like an eternity while I tried to hold her gaze, feeling smaller and smaller. "Sit down," she said finally with a glacial tone.

I lowered my eyes and quickly sat at the table. The girls followed and sat by my side, one on my left, one on my right, as Aunt Paulette lifted her chin and opened her arms. Charles threw himself against her with a muffled sob.

"My beautiful Baby," she said, softly patting his back with her good hand while her prosthetic hand moved clumsily back and forth without touching him. I saw Charles's head quiver as he carefully held his head away from his mother's shoulder so as not to smear make-up on her blouse. I wondered if he was crying.

"Don't pay attention to him. Do you hear? He is nothing," said Aunt Paulette through clenched teeth. She turned her face, dry and white, towards the sliding glass door. "Just look at him," she scoffed.

In the middle of the yard, the barefoot silhouette of my uncle stood under the pine tree. He smoked, looking down, back hunched as if supporting an unbearable invisible weight, his protruding stomach looking like a white bowling ball. With a heavy gesture, he brought the cigarette to his lips, took a long drag, then let his arm drop back down like something useless.

"Look at the cowboy," she said with a nervous snicker that spread quickly to Marie-Ange and Charles. I turned towards Stephanie, who glanced at me with confusion, hesitating, but then to my disappointment, she joined in the ridicule.

"Look at him now!" scowled Aunt Paulette.

I remained frozen, feeling sick to my stomach.

With a loud hiccup, Charles let go of his mother and sat down. His face was still perfectly made up, and for some reason he didn't look ridiculous anymore. Marie-Ange served the tea while my aunt lit a cigarette with her good hand, took it from her mouth, and placed it between two plastic fingers. The plate of cookies was passed around. In the silence, interrupted only by the clinking of silver spoons against porcelain cups and the monotonous clatter of the game analysts, they sipped tea. I didn't touch my cup, yearning for a cold soda that I was too intimidated to ask for.

"What is he doing now?" asked Aunt Paulette, craning her neck towards the backyard, blowing smoke.

"He's waving at the Mexicans," said Marie-Ange.

Uncle Larry was lifting a hand in a friendly gesture.

"I've told him over and over not to be nice to them," my aunt fumed. She hit the table with her prosthetic forearm and the ashes of her cigarette scattered over the white tablecloth. "Every time they have a get-together, they get drunk and play their mariachi late into the night. He's just encouraging them."

"He's going to see them," said Charles with alarm as his father walked away and disappeared from our field of vision.

"Drunk Mexicans. We never had that sort of problem in the Hills," said Aunt Paulette bitterly.

Charles got up in haste and stood in the middle of the living room. He peered through the glass with his mouth open, holding a cookie.

"Angie, do you remember the house in the Hills?" asked my aunt. "That big pool we had in the backyard? You must have been five or six. Do you remember?"

"He's talking to them," reported Charles, taking a bite out of the cookie. Crumbs fell from his mouth onto the carpet.

"I remember it was much nicer than this shithole," said Marie-Ange, slowly stirring her tea with a spoon.

"Please, watch your language," said my aunt sharply. "Don't you think I know that? If your father were not such a failure, we'd still live there."

"I don't remember anything about that house," said Stephanie.

Aunt Paulette turned her gaze back towards the empty yard and let out a snort. "He always has to be nice to everyone."

"One of them is giving him a beer," yelled Charles.

"He wants everyone to like him."

There was a pause, during which my aunt took a slow drag of her cigarette. Then she shook her head. "One day, they'll climb over the fence and attack us."

Marie-Ange's eyes shone. "And they'll probably try to rape us," she said.

Her mother raised a finger in the air and waved it back and forth. "Angie, I won't tolerate that sort of talk."

"They'll rape Stephie first," said Charles.

"Charles!" shouted Aunt Paulette, slamming the table hard with her forearm. The cigarette fell off and rolled on the tablecloth in a burst of sparks.

Stephanie tensed up and wrapped her arms around her torso. "Why me?" she cried.

"Yes, why her?" asked Marie-Ange, frowning.

My aunt was dipping her napkin into her teacup and dabbing at the incandescent ashes on the table.

"Because she is the pretty one," said Charles.

"You little asshole!" screamed Marie-Ange. She threw a spoon at him, which missed and bounced off the TV set with a clang.

I'd had enough. I stood up, knocking the chair backwards, and ran to the sliding door. In seconds, I slipped outside while Aunt Paulette furiously called my name. Skidding on the carpet of dead pine needles, I ran towards my uncle who was walking back, a red cup in hand. As I approached, I glanced at the men gathered behind the fence. Men with hard-lined sunburned faces and squinting eyes that I'd seen driving around in pickup trucks with tools rattling in the back but had never paid any particular attention to. There were no women among them.

"Uncle Larry," I said. I wanted to touch him and maybe hug him, but I stopped abruptly a few feet away.

"Little man," he said. He attempted to smile, only to display a weak grimace. He must have known what I was thinking. To hide his embarrassment, he took a long sip of beer, looking away.

Charles's whiny voice rose behind me. "Bobby, Maman wants you to come back in the house." He was standing outside, feet firmly planted, hands on his waist, puffing his chest with his chin high.

My uncle lowered his beer and opened his mouth but no sound came out of it. The men behind the fence fell quiet.

"I don't want tea," I said, my voice echoing in the sudden silence. "I hate tea."

"What are you doing, Charles?" Uncle Larry finally blurted. There was shuffling behind the fence, muttered words and repressed guffaws.

"Maman says Bobby needs to sit back at the table because he didn't ask to be excused."

"Get back in the house," said Uncle Larry with a voice that wanted to be firm but lacked authority, his eyes darting back and forth between his son and the neighbors.

All of a sudden, Charles's posture and colorful attire jolted my memory. Payback time, I thought. At the top of my lungs, I shouted, "Miss Piggy! Miss Piggy!" jumping in place and pointing at him. Then I made snorting sounds as loud as I could.

There was a brief confused silence during which my uncle looked at me with disappointed eyes. Then someone on the other side of the fence laughed and yelled, "Hola, Senorita Piggy." The man with the blue cap was brandishing a cup. Immediately, several men lifted their drinks and joyously parroted the salutation.

My uncle dropped his half-full cup of beer on the ground and walked briskly towards Charles. "Back inside!" he pleaded several times, wagging his finger, his tone getting more unsure as he got closer to him.

Charles stared in disbelief at the men hollering at him, ignoring his father. A boom box hung on the fence, and a young man with a black mustache turned the sound up. "Senorita Piggy! A bailar!" he yelled. Some of the men started to sway to the mariachi music with their arms in the air, yapping with excitement.

"Get him back in the house!" screamed Aunt Paulette from deep inside the living room.

"Please," implored Uncle Larry, trying to grab Charles by the shoulder, but with a swift move, my cousin escaped and ran several feet away. My uncle stood dumbfounded as his neighbors cheered and laughed. Charles puckered his lips and rolled his eyes. With a defiant frown, he paced back and forth, moving his hips with exaggeration from side to side, one hand behind his head, the other on his waist. "Que guapo maricón," someone said and the pack of men exploded in appreciative shouts and whistles, smacking their red cups together.

Uncle Larry ran in front of Charles, faced the neighbors, raised and waived his arms frantically, like someone on a highway trying to stop an oncoming truck. "Stop it!" he shouted. But the heckling, led by the man with the blue cap who, red-faced, slammed the fence excitedly with his fist, only swelled as Charles danced and lifted his skirt to show his legs, a crazed smile beaming on his face. "Stop it!" my uncle kept shouting without results, his voice cracking with increasing desperation. Then, Charles sang "La Cucaracha" with a high-strung falsetto voice and the men's laughter exploded.

"Are you going to do anything about this?" shrieked Aunt Paulette, peering out at the edge of the sliding door. "Anything at all?"

That was when my uncle turned and walked towards me. His eyes burned like red coals. I backed up in fright, but he continued past me in the direction of the toolshed. I watched him pull a set of keys out of his pocket, unlock the door and, seconds later, walk back, shotgun in hand. I closed my eyes, cold sweat pouring down my back, unable to move. A gust of air brushed my face as he strode by me, and I heard the determined shucking of the Mossberg 500.

Screams in Spanish erupted over the mariachi music. I waited for a blast, but nothing happened. I opened my eyes. Uncle Larry was standing there, legs apart, the shotgun against his chest, looking at the empty red cups rolling on the cement in the neighbor's yard. Meanwhile, Charles, his back turned, sang and shook his rump with hand moves as in Madonna's "Vogue" video, unaware his audience had scattered away.

"Not my Baby," cried out Aunt Paulette, bolting out of the living room as Uncle Larry took a step towards Charles. Tripping in her high heels but propelled by a savage force, she fell upon him and whacked the side of his head with her prosthetic arm. Mouth agape, my uncle stumbled back then regained his balance and, furrowing his eyebrows, raised the shotgun. There was a deafening bang and my aunt fell to the ground. Charles, who had just witnessed the scene, slapped his cheeks and uttered a prolonged, inarticulate squeal. Aunt Paulette, on her belly, squirmed on the carpet of pine needles. My uncle stood over her, the shotgun pointed at her head.

"Uncle Larry," I called out, running towards him. My fear had disappeared. I knew he wasn't going to hurt me.

Aunt Paulette rolled over, unharmed. The bullet had only shattered her artificial arm, now a bouquet of sharp plastic shards at the elbow. Her sunglasses had been knocked off, revealing her blind eye. Under a reddish eyelid, the white cornea without pupil peered at us. I recoiled, curling my lips. "Shoot me, but don't hurt him," she implored. "He's your son, for God's sake."

Uncle Larry shucked his gun.

With a gurgling yelp, Aunt Paulette buried her face under her stump. Charles stopped wailing and with a resigned but loud and clear voice said, "No, Papa. Kill me, Papa." He opened his arms wide, closed his eyes and offered his chest, inhaling deeply.

Uncle Larry turned his head and looked at me.

I shivered, reading for the first time in years a calm assurance in his pale blue eyes. He seemed taller and stronger and there was a faint smile at the corner of his mouth, as if he had it all figured out. For a fleeting instant he was, one last time, the cowboy on the billboard, his face full of dignified purpose and strikingly handsome.

He said, "Forgive me, little man. Better this way," and before I could say or do anything, he turned the shotgun around, dropped the butt to the ground, placed the muzzle against his heart, and leaning over it, pressed the trigger with his big toe.

COLLEGE LESSONS

Gabi Lorino

Within the Cal State University Northridge dorms, at the cafeteria, a rowdy bunch of guys saw me and my new friends from the all-female dorm and waved us over. My roommate Norma looked at me, smiled, shrugged, then walked over to their table; the rest of us followed.

We were new to the school. Freshmen. "Fresh meat," they called us. It wasn't so bad, really. We just had a lot to learn in a little bit of time. Including who was who.

I scanned the guys' faces after sitting down with my tray, which I'd filled with salad from the bar, a veggie burger, a plastic tumbler full of Dr. Pepper, and two servings of crisp French fries. Fellow students, as well as *Seventeen* magazine, had warned me about gaining the Freshman Fifteen, but I wasn't worried about that because the salad would balance things out.

It seemed impossible to remember everyone's names. Jerry was the dreamy half-Asian guy, but his background was different than Norma's, who was Filipina; I hoped his name would stick in my head. There were at least two Erics and three Mikes, however, and they sorted themselves out by last name or nickname. I couldn't remember all their stories and names, though.

Then there was the loud one: Leo. I looked at his partially shaved head, hoop earring in his left ear, golden tan, and impossibly white teeth. He looked like a Leo. Brash, loud, and funny; someone who was used to being the center of attention. Leo meant "lion," the king of the jungle. It followed that this guy had presence. I wondered if he was their de facto leader.

At first, he didn't pay much attention to me. I was more of a listener than a talker, so others grabbed the spotlight. Stories were exchanged of the where-are-you-from-what's-your-major variety. I was busy taking things in. As a scholarship student, living in the dorms was what I imagined life at a resort would be. Of course, I'd never been to a resort; my family didn't have the means to afford luxuries like that. I was surrounded by people who probably had more privilege and money than I, and it was embarrassing on one hand, fascinating on the other.

Across from me, one of the Erics concentrated on his slice of pizza and offered a polite smile when I looked over at him.

"It's like dinner theater," I said to him, nodding my head toward the others.

He laughed, and a few heads swiveled our way, including Leo's.

"What's so funny?" he asked.

"Nothing," I said. My heart beat faster as faces around the table goggled at me.

"It doesn't look like nothing," he added.

"We're just busy eating. That's all. Probably eating more than all of you, who are talking so much." I felt panicked, like I owed him an explanation. Then I wondered why I felt that way.

"Okay then." His voice had an edge to it, but then he shrugged and revisited the story he was telling about the low-budget film he made with his buddies.

The next day, as I walked between the buildings where I had classes, I heard a guy's voice calling, "Robin! Robin!" I turned around.

It was Leo with his dark shaved hair, in cargo pants and a baggy jacket, Coppertone tanned and smiling his perfect Leo smile. I sucked in a breath, flattered to be singled out; guys like that had never yelled for my attention before. I held up my hand to wave, and the next thing I knew, he was walking alongside me. "How's it going?" he asked. "I was just out here and I knew, just knew, you looked familiar, and I had to ask, did we tell you about our gig coming up?"

I blinked a few times, as if to clear my head, then tried to act as casual as I could. "I don't think so," I said.

"Three bands! They're letting us use the black box theatre. Should last about two hours. Eighteen and up, but they serve drinks in the lobby. Fake IDs welcome," he added with a nudge. "It's me, Eric Powell, Mike—you know, my roommate—and Doug on drums. You haven't met him yet, I don't think, but you will. Anyway, bring your friends! It'll be fun!"

"OK," I said as he held a flyer out for me to take. It was black ink on yellow paper.

"Take a few," he said, and when I complied, he smiled and dashed away.

Whew. The dude was intense—a hare to my tortoise. I was surprised he'd remembered my name, and very excited to be invited to see a band. It seemed like such a grown-up thing to do: to go see a band and not ask anyone for permission. Finally, I'd reached that stage when I wouldn't have to follow my parents' rules or follow a curfew anymore.

It turned out that the girls in my dorm didn't need much encouragement to attend an on-campus event that enabled us to do some secretive pre-drinking in our rooms.

"Guess who's the designated driver tonight? No one!" my roommate Norma squealed as we applied makeup in the mirror that hung on the wall between our twin beds, over our shared chest of drawers.

Our room was sparse, except for the smattering of posters we'd taped to the walls showcasing our favorite bands and the guys we wanted to look at all the time, like my personal favorite, Kurt Cobain. I couldn't wait to finally see Nirvana in concert, anywhere I could reach by car, but they weren't on any local concert listings. Rumor had it they were touring Europe.

"Do you think they'll be any good?" I asked Norma as I applied black eyeliner.

"Let's see, they've been playing together for five months? Probably not." She laughed and searched her backpack for her lipstick, applied it, then pulled a tissue from a box to blot it.

I considered what to wear. "Just anything black should work, huh?" I asked.

She nodded, then added, "No mini-skirts. Remember those creepy frat guys?"

I considered myself in the mirror. I'd chopped most of my hair off, but with the help of some gel and a few tricks with the hair dryer, it stuck out in the right places—at least, for the moment. The dye job Norma had helped with had turned it several shades darker than I'd anticipated, but I hoped it gave me the look of someone creative and introspective. In the back of my mind was the worry of what my conservative family would think, but I had until Thanksgiving to find that out.

I wore my black combat boots, obviously, with jeans and a long-sleeved black blouse and some silver jewelry. I wanted my look to say, "I'm cool, but I'm also into dudes." Having shorter hair gave me confidence in some situations and made me feel wildly insecure in others.

After our next-door neighbor Melanie knocked on our door, we took off on foot with a smattering of others from our floor. We were a band of sisters guilty of tipsiness but having enough collective self-preservation to travel together to our destination, fresh from the admonishing talks about campus safety. It occurred to my beer-altered mind that we were dodging rapists lurking in the shadows while on a trek to meet cute guys that we might hook up with later. Guys, like experiences, weren't interchangeable.

Shadows trailed behind our giggling mass as our footsteps echoed throughout the campus. It looked much different at night. Light posts that I never noticed in the daytime took center stage. Darkness lingered in places that were usually lit up by the beaming sun in a cloudless sky.

We soon found ourselves surrounded by grad students, faculty, and fellow undergrads in the theater lobby. Our laughter mixed with the boring talk of professors, and when the theater doors opened, we tumbled in to sit on U-shaped bleachers in the low light.

The Wanderers went on first. This was Leo's band, and an ironic name because he was a townie, born and raised in L.A. I wasn't sure about the other guys, though.

The lights came up. Leo was the lead singer, naturally, and he had his back to the audience ... well, a third of the audience. We saw his profile. Norma glanced away, then tapped my arm and pointed at girls our age gaping over the guys, or maybe just Leo. She flipped her hair behind her shoulder, then elbowed me and whispered, "Groupies, they've got groupies."

I laughed and whispered back, "Yet we manage to keep our clothes on around them."

She giggled.

With the spotlight on him, Leo moved, shook, and gestured along with his words. At one point, he spun and shook on the stage, which had an aphrodisiac effect on the ladies near us but gave Norma and me the giggles. Their last number, a cover of the Doors' "Light My Fire," had him writhing onstage. This won him the frenzied cheers from the audience while I exchanged alarmed glances with Norma. She whispered to me, "Close your eyes and think of Kurt."

We had to wait a while to congratulate them after the show, but when we did, I noticed Leo's measured glance at me, as if signaling his approval.

Later that night, he called up to our room from the dorm telephone outside and we snuck him upstairs through the side doors. We had to do this: visiting hours were over and guys weren't allowed in our rooms.

After following our lead and tiptoeing down the hallway, his voice regained its pitch when our dorm room door was closed. "Tonight was EPIC!" he said.

"Shhhhhhh!" I said while Norma gave him a shocked look.

"Dude, the RA is *right down the hall*," she hissed.

"Sorry," he said, then grinned sheepishly. Leo toured my side of our room, looking at the posters I'd hung, nodding in approval of my choices. Then, he dropped down onto my bed and patted the bed next to him, gazing at me with puppy-dog eyes.

I'd planned to sit on my desk chair, not next to him. Not on a bed.

Yes, he was the lead singer and everyone thought he was attractive, but something was off. Girls like me didn't end up with the lead singer. We ended up with posters of the lead singer.

I knew it would make things awkward — scratch that, more awkward — if I didn't sit next to him. Even though it felt odd. So I did, though I couldn't uncross my arms.

Norma fussed at the mirror, pulled off her necklace, and unlaced her boots. "Fun time tonight," she said. "When are you guys playing out again?"

Leo rattled off some dates coming up, closer to the holidays, then elbowed me. "You'll be there, right?" he asked.

"Of course," I said. "We'll come whenever we can."

"Good, good," he replied.

Our phone rang and I jumped. Norma, whose bed was next to it, answered it, smiled, and hung up soon after.

"Jay's downstairs," she said. "We're going to run around for a while." She looked down at her stockinged feet and frowned, then began the arduous process of putting her Doc Martens back on.

Meanwhile, Leo's hand snaked around me and settled on my waist.

I wished Norma would stay. How had I ended up like this? And what did it say about me, that I was filled with more foreboding than excitement? Girls my age went crazy when they went away to school, especially when it came to drinking and boys. This was my first time alone with a boy since senior prom, and I was nervous as hell. Was something wrong with me?

I forced a smile when Norma got up to leave, jingling her keys in her hand and quipping, "Don't wait up! I can let myself in!"

"She's really cool," Leo said after the door closed behind Norma.

"Yeah, I like living with her. She's cool," I added.

"So."

"Um."

He was giving me that look. That I'm-going-to-kiss-you look — I could tell even when it was in my peripheral vision and partially shrouded by his shaggy bangs.

I turned and looked at him, closing my eyes despite an odd heavy feeling in my belly. The kiss was inevitable. And mechanical, I realized after it began. Where was the chemistry? It was a firm, skilled kiss, but it lacked that essential element.

He gently tried to ease me back so that we'd end up lying on the bed. Unlike before, though, I pushed away and slid to the edge of the bed. Heat flooded my face and must have raised the temperature of my dorm room five degrees.

"I'm so sorry," I said, placing my warm face in my hands. "I'm so embarrassed."

"Don't be," he said, patting my back.

"I'm —"

I sensed some anger in him, as though he was doing and saying things to come off as sensitive, but it didn't seem genuine.

But how could I say I wasn't interested? How could anyone not be interested in Leo? I didn't want him to get mad, or to force anything with me.

Everything inside me said no to him; our brief kiss had told me that. Besides, I had no experience at all beyond my high school boyfriend.

"I'm a virgin," I blurted.

Then I saw a flicker of understanding in his eyes. Nobody messed with a virgin unless he wanted to be her boyfriend and hang around for months and months, exclusively dating her. That was the rule, wasn't it?

"No worries," he said, then stood to look out my window.

I silently sighed in relief and did my best to keep the conversation going, feeling responsible for his bruised ego. I took on a humble tone and said, "I'm surprised that you'd come here tonight. Of all the people at your show, I thought Melanie was more your speed."

Our neighbor Melanie was blonde and curvy. Hot, really.

"She's a bit preppy," he said after crossing his arms.

I heard what he was saying. He wanted someone edgy, like me. Dark hair, dark clothes, into progressive music. But it wasn't going to be me.

"You know, we *just* got here," I said, pointing out the window at campus. "There are so many adventures to be had. And your band? Your band's got a lot of fun gigs ahead."

This was my way of saying *let's just be friends*, without saying, "Let's just be friends."

It was a good segue to other topics, like Nirvana's latest album, how to earn college credit for going scuba diving in Mexico, and Leo's guitar lessons. We were sprawled on the floor reading the liner notes from my CDs, which I stored in a Converse All-Stars box, when Norma knocked and then walked in.

"Have fun?" I asked.

She giggled and flopped down on her bed.

"I should go," Leo said, and I nodded. I escorted him down the hall to the exit and opened it quietly, then closed it after him.

Once he was gone, I told Norma about our awkward kiss. We came up with a safe word to use in case we had future situations in which we didn't want to be left alone. After that, it was basically forgotten.

And anyway, despite — or maybe because of — my lack of chemistry with Leo, we were "in" with him and the band.

Our corkboard collected a flurry of flyers throughout freshman year. Parties, shows, and other special events enhanced Norma's and my new college life.

She and I regrouped for Year Two after spending our summers away. She worked in her family's restaurant in Alhambra, while I worked at a mall in Bakersfield near my parents' house and helped out around our farm. Our dorm setup was more or less the same, and we saw most of the Mikes and Erics at the cafeteria again, but Leo was gone.

Eric Powell, also known as Skater Eric, told us that Leo's parents had helped Leo buy a house in North Hollywood. He'd recruited Doug, the drummer, as a roommate.

It was a gritty place with a shiny name. Gritty or not, though, how lucky was he to have a house?

"Bring me meat!" Leo proclaimed from Norma's and my shared answering machine, once we had re-connected by telephone. He provided his new address and basic directions to his house. The barbecue that he hosted allowed us to reunite with the past year's crowd. Though Norma and I were chided for bringing salad to share, they ate every bit of it.

Leo's backyard was desolate: leaves on top of dry dirt. Plastic chairs were strewn about, and a concrete wall divided his property from his neighbors'. He and his roommate Doug had heard gunshots from the backyard, and that, he said, was why he planned to host only barbecues. Less shady things happened in the daylight.

Two hours into any get-together, he was always drunk. Inspired by a *Simpsons* episode, Leo sang, "You can't make friends with salad," over and over while he hung his arm around my shoulders outside by the grill. I noticed a sidelong glance from a woman he'd invited.

I elbowed him and said, "You're drunk, dude."

I saw his eyes dart over to her, and then he took his hand away after giving my waist a squeeze. I was too busy rolling my eyes to look over at her. Maybe she looked sufficiently jealous at that point, I don't know. Whatever was happening, it wasn't cool.

Once we'd loaded up our plates with burgers, dogs, and side dishes, Doug sat between me and Norma and asked us about school. When I started to reply, Leo yelled, "Is that a dead squirrel hanging out of Doug's shirt?" and laughed loudly. "Oh wait, no, it's just his hairy gut."

Doug looked away and pulled his sweatshirt down over his waistband.

"Leo, cut that out," I said.

"What's your deal?" Norma added.

Doug gave me a hollow look, but said nothing.

I noticed that Doug didn't seem to relax that afternoon at all. Leo was constantly chiding him. I knew from other parties that Doug was a lot more interesting than Leo was, but apparently Leo couldn't help it. He had to grab the spotlight.

Leo went inside, and conversation returned to normal. When he returned, his acoustic guitar in hand, I knew it wasn't for a singalong. It was time for another performance.

Doug slipped away, and I dutifully remained in my chair for Leo's show. He went through the college essentials — Bob Marley, The Cure, and The Police — and asked me at the end, "Did I sound good? I mean, really good?"

What the hell could I say, aside from, "Yes, of course!" like an idiot fangirl. If he needed adulation, he should have asked the woman he was ignoring instead of me.

His performance was all right. No goosebumps were raised. I didn't feel moved by the music, much like that kiss we'd shared my freshman year, a kiss that I was happy to forget.

I snuck inside to use the bathroom and got caught up in a conversation with Doug. He'd landed a sought-after internship as a videographer for a local news channel, which was a huge deal in the L.A. market.

"I'm really happy for you," I said. Behind him, a muted TV played music videos.

He nodded and smiled.

I liked Doug. There was something about him that was calm, different, easygoing. He stood about six feet tall and was heavier than the rest of the guys in the band. He looked like a generic white guy from a distance, but up close his blue eyes were bright and engaging.

Doug seemed smart, and unlike Leo and the other music/film guys, he actually worked and went to school. There was nothing more annoying to me than a pampered student with no job who complained to me about being a "poor college student." So what if he didn't have a smooth washboard stomach like Leo? Doug was a real person.

I wasn't bold enough to ask him out, and he seemed shy too. Sure, I had his phone number — it was Leo's number too — but it felt like I wasn't allowed to explore my little crush, not with Leo around. In addition, telling Leo about it would have invited bad behavior that I couldn't predict. It was as if Leo was in charge and the rest of us were pawns. He'd place us where he wanted: in the audiences of his gigs, at the liquor store picking up the kegs for his parties, and sitting around his backyard, laughing at his jokes. Such was the strength of his personality.

At Leo's next party — "Bring me meat! I'll give you meat to put in your mouth!" he had bellowed into our answering machine — Doug was absent.

"What happened to Doug?" I asked.

Skater Eric locked eyes with mine and shook his head.

"That guy's so fucking lame," Leo said. "He just ditched. Such a loser."

After a few murmurs that didn't provide an explanation, I let the issue drop, sat down with my food, listened to the music, and did my best to look entertained. I slipped inside to use the bathroom and heard Leo say, through the back door, "No, he sucked as a roommate. I need to get some women in here that I can control."

My eyes went wide. Wow. It was 1994 and guys still talked like that? Out loud?

I opened the back door loudly, knowing that he wouldn't have wanted his previous comment to be overheard by someone like myself, a member of the "weaker sex."

"Hey, Robin!" Leo said, greeting me with an easy smile as I walked outside.

"Hey, Leo! I've gotta go. My shift starts in an hour. But thanks for having me." I didn't usually lie to my friends, but this seemed like the right time to start, because I could imagine what was coming out of his mouth next.

"Yeah! Always a pleasure! Hey, when you and Norma move out of the dorms, let's talk. I've got some space, would love to have you two here."

My insides lurched. "Ah," I said, aiming for a neutral expression. Never had my face betrayed my gut this much. I might have lied to my parents about where my friends and I were going on a Saturday night back in high school, but I'd never had cause to lie to my friends before. "You know we have to stay close to campus. Work's taking over our lives!"

"But seriously, I'd make you a deal!" he said.

"Let's talk later. Sorry, gotta go. Bye guys!"

Leo clasped me into a hug before letting me go, probably to further piss off the woman he was ignoring. I realized, too late by this point, that I should have advised her to talk to other guys. That would've guaranteed her instant attention from Leo.

Over Leo's shoulder, Skater Eric gave me a glance that said, "We'll talk later."

I winked at him and walked through the house to the safety of my car, sighing when I got inside and started the engine.

Norma's reaction of, "Oh, yeah, right!" came after I explained the Leo-needing-female-roommates-he-could-control situation. "No way no how. Tell him we're not going to do it."

"He won't be so easy to convince. And what if he gets mad?" I asked.

"Why do we have to be polite?" Norma's eyes were wide and wild. "Why do we have to pretend that we care about his feelings? The guy's a misogynist leech!"

"I know," I said. I didn't know how to break away from him, even though I knew it would be better if I did.

The answering machine messages that followed stressed me out. We weren't answering our phone anymore, but we did pick up while the answering machine ran if we wanted to talk to whoever was leaving a message.

"Ladies. Lay-DEES! Leo here. Wanted to talk to you, Robin, and NORMA!" He called out Norma's name like the cast of *Cheers* called out "Norm." "When's your lease up? When can you move in? Let's dialogue."

"I don't want anything to do with him! I'm not living with him," Norma repeated. "I don't know about you," she added, pointedly looking at me with her arms crossed.

My insides felt heavy. "Of course I'm not either."

"Then why are you stringing him along?"

"I'm not!" I insisted. "I keep telling him no, and he keeps overriding me."

"Maybe he'll figure out you're not moving in when you don't move in with him."

"Yeah, it seems like that's the only way he's going to understand."

Norma and I signed a lease at an apartment complex about a mile from campus. The apartments were brick with wooden staircases and iron railings: cozy, cute, and convenient to work and school. It wasn't too expensive, and there were more families there than students, so it would be quiet. The opposite of Leo's place.

With the lease signed, I felt safely insulated from Leo, so I called him to tell him about the apartment. "Hey there. Yeah. We'll be off campus nearby. Just like I already told you, Leo! I told you I couldn't manage the drive to your place, not with my old car. It takes money to buy a new one, you know! Yeah, shut up."

Leo said he was up for a part in a short film, which would take up all his time. "Yeah, I told the guys that we should disband for a while."

I smirked, glad that we were talking on the phone instead of in person. There had to be more to this story, but I wasn't about to ask Leo about it. "Sounds great! College is all about new experiences."

The disbanding came at the right time for me, because I wanted to limit my time around Leo. That would allow me to pursue my other friendships with the guys as well as continue to enjoy Norma's company in a stress-free way. This was my way of saying *let's hang out with other people* without saying, "Let's hang out with other people."

When I hung up, I looked at the digital display on my clock radio, rallied a sleeping Norma, and led her downstairs and to the cafeteria.

Skater Eric and a few of the Mikes were there. After loading up my tray, I plopped down at their table and said, "Okay, guys, spill. What happened to the band?"

Skater Eric stroked his goatee and then laughed. "Well, it all started with Doug," he said. "Wait, first of all, you're not moving in with him, are you?"

One of the Mikes, Blond Mike, laughed. "Yeah, poor Doug."

"No! God no!" Norma interjected, then went back to eating her lasagna.

"Okay, okay," Skater Eric said, "so Doug had a long-distance love interest. I wouldn't say girlfriend, but heading that way. Anyway, she came to visit, and Leo. Well, you know Leo."

"That dude does not know when to back off," Blond Mike said.

"What an ass," Norma said. "Did he get very far with her?"

"Not really, but she's the kind of person, you know, the kind who doesn't want to be rude, and since Leo's talking to her, she feels obliged to listen, and meanwhile, the weekend's just flying by, and Doug's getting pushed to the side."

"Good God, that's exactly me," I said. "Getting stuck because I don't want to be rude."

"So, Doug finally gets her out of there, and they go stay in a hotel so they can have some peace and quiet."

"Oh my God, seriously?" I asked. "That costs money. Like, grown-up money."

"So uncool," Blond Mike said.

Skater Eric continued. "So, after she left, Doug told him no more cockblocking, no more band, and I'm moving out. That left us looking at each other like, 'Do we want to keep playing with Leo? Do *any* of us want to live with him?' And we were like, um no."

"Yeah, us too," Norma said, then took a sip of Coke.

"I mean, he sells tickets. Girls love him. But it's just bad mojo."

"He made it sound like it was his idea to break up the band, right?" Blond Mike added, then burst out laughing when I nodded.

I didn't see Leo for a while after that. At first I played nice when he called, claiming a hefty work schedule, but after Kurt Cobain died, I pretty much shut down. Yes, I knew it was a fantasy, but Kurt had seemed so gentle, so funny, so smart and wonderful, and though it was unlikely that we would have ever met, it still felt like a part of me left when he died.

Still, I functioned on autopilot, went to work and school, bought stuff for our new place. When we picked up the keys for our apartment right before Finals Week, our lives became a flurry of moving and studying.

Clean laundry was heaped on top of my bed, and I folded while Norma sped in and out of the dorm room, carrying loads of books and seldom-worn clothes to her car. I propped the door open for her convenience and occasionally waved to a neighbor who walked down the hall.

We were using black garbage bags for transporting most of our clothes, and as I filled a bag with sweaters, sweatshirts, and other items that were useless in the eighty-degree heat, a deep voice boomed down the hallway. "Robin! She who *still* hasn't called me back!"

I winced, then forced a smile when Leo stuck his head in the doorway and peered into my room. His hair had grown longer and was dyed blue-black, contrasting with his permanently tanned skin.

"Hey, Leo, how's it going?" I managed.

"Where'd ya go, Leo?" Hot Melanie from next door asked, then sidled near him so that he would drape his arm around her when she fit herself neatly next to him. She wore more make-up than usual and more than was necessary. Probably to impress Leo, I thought.

"Hey Mel," I added, then shook out a new bath towel, folded it into eighths, and added it to the black bag.

"I can't believe you didn't come to my last party. Does this thing still work?" Leo asked, motioning toward the white plastic answering machine on Norma's side of the room.

"Oh that," I said, then managed a tight smile. "I'm not a carefree, job-free freshman anymore, Leo. You know that."

"Yeah, you need money for your new place, huh?" The edge to his voice grew sharper.

I did my best to ignore it. "Among other things, yeah."

"When's the housewarming?" Melanie asked.

I shrugged and saw, over her shoulder, Norma approach our doorway and then quickly retreat. Her eyes were wide with alarm; I knew she didn't want to see Leo again.

"Yeah! Seriously! Seems like I'm always the one throwing the parties," Leo added.

"I can let you both know once we're settled," I said, though I told myself that I didn't have to make myself do it. I was adhering to social niceties, much like grown-ups who said, "Let's do lunch," and never followed through on it.

"You got a phone installed yet?" Leo asked.

I shook my head. That was true.

"When you're set up over there, you owe me a phone call. I'm serious, I keep score, and it's *your* turn to call *me*." Then he laughed and jostled Melanie playfully as if he were joking. She responded by grabbing him around his waist, and then her hand descended lower, passing over the fabric of his jeans.

I folded another towel and put on my best placating tone. "Sounds like a plan."

Kurt Cobain posthumously added to the conversation by singing "Something in the Way" from my nearby boom box.

"And how the hell is Norma?" Leo barked while Melanie pulled him back to her room by two belt loops.

"She's good. Super busy," I answered.

"Gotta go. See you this summer, yeah?" Leo said as he disappeared from the doorway.

"Take care, Leo," I said.

Why did I feel guilty about our interaction? I just wanted him to leave me alone.

It probably had to do with Bakersfield. Lots of people shudder when they hear "Bakersfield," but it was where I grew up, regardless. Bakersfield was much different from L.A. or even Northridge. "Family-friendly" was a term they threw around a lot there, and boy, did they mean it! Church, family, and community ties had kept me "in line" for my first eighteen years. My strategy of getting awesome grades and never getting into trouble had helped me escape living there, but I had to wonder: Had saying yes-ma'am-no-ma'am-yes-sir-no-sir too many times programmed me to give my attention to whomever demanded it the most, even though that gave Leo an unfair advantage and completely wore me out?

Before, when my friends had tolerated Leo, it had been too easy to wear blinders. Sure, he'd used me to make other women jealous. When Leo manipulated the wording of a question to get the answer he wanted, I'd always given the "right" answer, even if it wasn't honest. It was easier to just go along with what he wanted and what the strength of his personality demanded, even though it diminished my integrity.

Norma and I were both home at the apartment when the phone company guy came to install our telephone line, and she insisted that the phone be billed under her name.

"It's better if you, uh, well, since you're a woman," the man mumbled as he looked at the yellow copy of his service order on his clipboard.

Norma cut him off. "We've heard the safety talk already. We won't be listing our number in the phone book, and we're going to be *really* selective about who we give this number to." She raised her eyebrows at me as if to say, "This is what we're doing."

We hadn't talked about Leo for a while, though the implication that we were "women he could control" had sent her into a spin. I remembered her saying, "You're from the country, and I'm Filipina. Does that mean we have no minds of our own? That we can be controlled by a man? That we can't live on our own, without a man, during our *peak party years?*"

That was the moment I wondered if my hollow feeling was the result of his manipulative oppression, cleverly disguised as friendship. Maybe it wasn't my feelings of obligation that kept my stomach churning; maybe Leo was doing that, just by being Leo.

I nodded at Norma and the telephone guy, though the heavy feeling remained. She was right, of course. No matter how guilty I felt about abandoning someone, I couldn't keep putting up with Leo because that was what he wanted. There had to be more to life than that.

It was like "The Sweater Song" by Weezer. He'd pulled one thread, and everything started to unravel. First Doug, then the band, then Norma and me. We all needed to move on. What was it I'd said? "College is all about having new experiences!"

Besides, my studies were getting more challenging. Instead of taking the music/film route like Leo and those of his echelon, I was in the College of Business and Economics studying statistics instead of musical scales, learning to forecast trends instead of schmoozing. What I was studying seemed a lot more tangible — and boring — than their endeavors, but it was more likely to provide me with a real future.

☾

Norma and I reluctantly found new living arrangements after graduation because we found jobs on opposite sides of L.A., and I lost track of the guys except for Eric Powell (formerly Skater Eric), who was now my boyfriend, when my entry-level job took over most of my waking hours. My focus shifted from college to building my quote-un-quote adult life.

The higher-ups at my company didn't understand work-life balance, but they did respect our schedules when we enrolled in school. That was one reason I eventually signed up for a night class to learn HTML. Every Tuesday, after slipping away from the office mid-afternoon, I headed east to a nearby community college where I would change into comfortable clothes, grab an early dinner, sprawl out on the lawn with my books, and study before class. It was a welcomed break from overtime.

During my commute, the interstate bottlenecked at one bend in the road. It wasn't too terrible by L.A. standards, but it did delay me a while each week.

I generally ran the air conditioner, but the way the air felt on a November Tuesday was irresistible. I cracked the windows and opened my sunroof, knowing that, aside from the gridlock, it could be a pleasant drive ahead.

When red brake lights lit up in front of me, I slowed down. I thought I heard someone yelling my name as I inched forward, but I shook my head. Who would do that?

I heard my name again, a piercing shout against the hum of cars around me. Whoever it was sounded crazed, so I sealed up my windows, closed the sunroof, and turned on the air conditioner.

In my peripheral vision, someone bounced in a nearby car's driver's seat and waved at me while honking the horn repeatedly. His car windows were halfway down.

"Robin!" The man's ragged, manic voice came in clearer. It was Leo's.

I looked straight ahead. God only knew why he was yelling for me, why his need for attention was so great, and what his deal was after the six years I'd left him alone.

At first, I thought I might rebound into my old pattern of gut-wrenching submissiveness, but I took in three long, deep breaths, like I'd practiced in yoga class, and felt a strange numbness.

Acknowledging Leo wasn't an option; it would only encourage him. I'd learned that the hard way. I had to feign ignorance — and deafness — to protect myself. I'd placed years and miles between us, and I'd disappeared from his life to improve my own. To feel better in my own skin.

I kept my head facing forward, but noticed my neck muscles weren't tense, like I'd assumed they might be. Tilting my head to the side, away from him, I stretched my neck and yawned. The traffic in front of me inched forward, and I moved my car, then realized that the gnawing in my belly hadn't returned. This man who had once tried to seduce me, who fed off my attention like a vampire fed off blood, was now reduced to a desperate man yelling on a California highway. I felt sorry for him, like you might feel sorry for a crazy person.

A memory popped into my head, from the year Eric and I got together, back in Norma's and my first apartment. Eric played a song for me on his guitar and then said, "I'm not going to ask you if this is really great. I want you to tell me what you really think about it. It's a work in progress."

That gesture — of not being put on the spot, of not being guided toward what to say, of being given the freedom to think, judge, comment, and use my own mind — had made me feel more at ease than I ever had around a guy before. I'd lived in a world of parroting back what family members and professors and peers wanted to hear — when I was given permission to speak — but Eric gave me the space to think for myself. That was what made him the obvious choice for my First Grown-Up Boyfriend.

Of course, through his own selfish ways, Leo had unwittingly driven this point home too.

I kept my eyes on the road in front of me as I drove forward again. Leo now spoke loudly into a cell phone, self-importantly broadcasting his business to all within earshot. I turned up the volume on my car stereo to hear a mixed CD that Eric had made for me. Foo Fighters' "Monkey Wrench" filled the space inside my car, and soon I was singing along with it.

Once the traffic started to flow, I continued onward in search of a street vendor to get some dinner. The sun set behind me as I moved in fits and starts toward my next lesson.

FACE

Cody Sisco

Worse than losing myself in the crowd, worse than becoming an afraid-lonely-miserable hipster hermit living in poverty jammed up alongside ridiculously wealthy and shallow bling-clad influencer fruitnuts, worse than that was this: becoming ensnared when I least expected it.

Ensnared. A hideous word.

And the worst was that I didn't want to find my way out again.

The first sign of trouble: a horn blaring from a pick-up truck behind me, which should have snapped me out of the daze. Deep in traffic where brake lights flared and dimmed, driving to work, I reached a breaking point. That horn was the first of many warning signals that failed to register as I slipped deeper into the trap of obsession.

I leaned forward in my seat and stared at a face floating high above the 110, pasted on the side of an overpass. I couldn't tell if it was a man or a woman, and I didn't really care. My only enduring sexual preference has been an aversion to extremes of gender expression. The eyes were wide ovals, unnaturally white, like hard-boiled eggs. A suggestion of cheekbones, thin lips. It wasn't an Instagrammable face. It didn't inspire lust, not on first glance, only longing, and a tickly feeling in my brain like the hybrid baby of déjà vu and a forgotten word.

The face was printed on vinyl, perhaps, or silkscreened cloth, affixed to the underside of an overpass that was impossible to reach, not without rappelling down, hovering above ten lanes of traffic, and somehow swooping back toward the support pillar, requiring Cirque du Soleil levels of acrobaticism to pull off. New apartments lined the freeway, a meandering river cutting through a canyon of building-block toyland that makes up downtown L.A. How many glances skimmed that face as it was maneuvered into place, how many hundreds? And yet I hadn't seen it on my feeds.

The horn blared again, three long whines in succession, but they sounded far away, tinny, like an EDM bro on the Metro blasting tracks on a smartphone speaker the size of a bead. Sometimes that EDM bro had been me; I'd earned the nickname Speakerfucker back when I was still doing Molly, before the tinnitus began.

Above the freeway, the face stared at me — a snapshot in time, in gilded exhaust-leavened morning light. The face stared at *me*.

I'd noticed during my time commuting in L.A. that distance could take on different flavors. Bitter separation. Fond longing. Sexual tautness. Looking up at those eyes, the need I felt, the unmatched, cavernous desperation, it yanked something loose inside me that had been tightly wound, a dangerous unspooling.

The only time I recalled feeling exactly that way was the moment I confessed my love, my need, to my best friend in middle school. I watched his face crumple and twist with feelings that didn't need to be named in order to be understood. He revolted. In a moment, separation breached our friendship. He drew away. I could not let go. My longing, my desperate, self-effacing, self-harming hunger as I looked up at the face above the pavement was the same.

The fast lane in front of me, which had been creeping along in a snaking line of red brake lights since it came shuddering to a crawl at the heights of Elysian Park, was empty for about 100 yards. I should have moved. I should have pressed the accelerator. Instead, I put the car in park and slapped the button to turn on my hazards; their *click-click click-click* provided a metronome to my swirling thoughts and circling questions.

Whose face was it? Who put it there? Peering up, I saw that a few tightly curving ramps above the traffic would block most drivers' views of the face. I was in the narrow band of road where it was visible. Going the other direction, someone might glimpse it in their rearview, guileless eyes, dispassionate, watching the road with as much interest as I watched ants trekking across the parking lot at work while I sat on the curb with my vape.

A loud knock on my window, knuckles rapping on glass, finally roused me. My heart slammed in my chest, and I took a shuddering breath. In the rearview mirror, I saw that my lips were blue, my eyes spooked wide. The truck behind me also had its hazards on. Looming on my left, a figure leaned in, a plaid shirt, age-worn jeans. My hands gripped the steering wheel so tight they ached, its ridges pressed into my fingers.

"Are you okay?"

Weeks prior, stuck in the same jam, before I noticed the face or before it was there, I'd had a vision of being carjacked, my body — strangely paralyzed and limp — had been dragged from the car and beaten. Witnesses watched sidelong, grateful it wasn't them. A stranger calmly took the wheel of my car, smug and satisfied to see the traffic flow resume and a pile of flesh in the narrow median recede.

Now, having seen the face, I knew I wouldn't go gently to such a fate. Surrounded by glinting metal, mirrored glass, fumes, and dust, and a few improbable hardy palms defying a cityscape that seemed intended to compartmentalize, contain, and control life in all its forms, I had a purpose. I steeled myself for an altercation.

The question was echoed: "Are you okay?"

I didn't answer. The face stared down at me; a question infused its gaze: Would you give up yourself to find me?

A deeper voice, the one I heard late at night telling me to drive, to get out of town, to find a desolate wasteland, and to walk until the end of the earth, told me what to do. I was in L.A. after all, a place that encouraged self-deception.

I eased the car forward. The plaid-and-denim-wearing man watched for a moment, then turned back to his truck. I edged lane by tedious lane to the right, caught the 3rd Street exit, and parked on the frontage road in a red zone next to a small lot for city vehicles. I got out and looked back. The rise of the hill flanking downtown blocked my view of the face. I was thinking about skirting the fence around the parking lot, weaving through the tents and makeshift shelters perched on the hillside above the freeway, trying to find my way back to a view of the face when my phone bleeped the opening notes of "Take on Me."

I snapped out of it, laughing to myself. *Wow, could I be a spazz sometimes. I'm glad that's over.*

My phone screen showed a text from Alea saying she'd be fifteen minutes late and could I open the register? I knew she'd be handing off her toddler girl to her grandmother, the three of them an interlocking cooperative of women who faced far more problems in a year than I'd ever face in a lifetime.

No problem, I replied. Then I checked Waze and saw that she still might beat me there. I cut across to Union, then Hoover, and made it to the bookstore late but first to arrive.

All through my shift, the shape of the face hovered before me wherever I looked. I became convinced it was the face of someone I'd seen before, but I couldn't pin down who.

Alea handled restocking and tackling the new shipment from a self-help publisher while I sat at the counter, staring into space. We usually didn't get more than one or two customers before noon. People could get every book we sold online at a third of the price or better. We stayed in business on the merchandise.

Alea let me zone out for an hour and then, fed up with my inaction, summoned me to break down the boxes she emptied.

"More white-guy advice," Alea said as she removed four slim hardcover volumes of mindfulness quackery from a cardboard box. "Bestseller, you think?" she asked, her voice steeped in loathing.

"Better than Deepak," I said. "Look at this man's gorgeous hair." The cover showed a kindly face below a polished bald crown.

She snorted. "The Goop recipe book sells better, I bet."

In the afternoon, I took down every photography book from the shelves, looked at their covers, and flipped through each of them, looking for that face. It had to be a promotional thing, someone trying to drum up some street buzz, so maybe it was a rehash of a famous photo portrait. Or maybe, given the emo-intensity of the look, maybe it was a music thing. But there had been nothing to go on that was associated with the face: no number, no website, no social media handle. I slammed the last book shut so hard that Alea came by, looking at me skeptically with one eye narrowed, the other under a raised eyebrow. "Thought I heard a gunshot."

"Yes. I just killed myself out of boredom."

"Cool. Long as I don't have to clean up the mess." Her gaze flicked across my face. "Are you okay?"

I shrugged, feeling in that moment that I was the embodiment of effete nihilism.

"You want to close early? Grab a drink?" she asked.

"Maybe."

We had twenty minutes until official closing time, but the boss was in Italy doing research to gauge the effects of cheese and wine on his heart condition. We locked up and stood outside, roasting on the sidewalk in the full, heavy heat of mid-July.

"Drink?" she asked, feigning interest in furthering our friendship. She had friends, a family, made too many plans and canceled half of them every day — a busy life. I didn't have that problem. I was a recovering party boy turned book nerd that she felt sorry for and made a minimal effort to coax out of his shell. She examined her nails, painted shimmering turquoise at the base with glittering green tips that reminded me of Disney fish colors and underseascapes. "You got something on your mind," she noted.

"Tomorrow, maybe," I said. "I've got to run."

"Grindr date?" she asked.

"Yep," I lied.

"Let me know when you're ready for some chocolate with your strawberry."

"Ravish me, dark lady!" I knew for a fact that I was too spindly and malnourished-looking for her tastes and, furthermore, she'd disavowed men after baby daddy said bye-bye. Between us there wasn't a genital we liked in common.

She smiled and winked. "Good luck on your date. I want to hear all about it."

On the drive home, I lurched north in traffic, checking my rearview as I passed through the DTLA bottleneck, but I didn't see the face. I don't know whether it was the angle or the fading light. I took the 101 north and exited onto Echo Park Ave, doubled back, and approached the overpass on Temple. This time I was blocked by the 110 south. I drove around in the dark, going slowly, getting honked at every couple minutes by legitimately angry drivers and stared at by people on the street shuffling their shopping carts back to their patches of asphalt or sidewalk for the night. I knew I looked *off*. Everyone was on edge. The Skid Row killings had made the news the previous week and another body had washed up in Venice two days before. Someone was stalking the homeless, which made my innocent quest look suspicious.

I gave up at 10 p.m., scarfed tacos from a truck in Glassell Park, and drove up San Fernando. The room I rented in a guest house also had a place to park. It was worth every penny I couldn't afford.

I fell asleep in my hot, dank room, and woke at 3 a.m., an erection trapped against rough, borrowed sheets. Everything in my life was on loan, begged for, or otherwise tenuous. My job came through the generosity of a gender studies professor who always asked if I had enough to eat. My car was leased from a student who was studying in China for the semester. This room was an affordable, karmic gift from an elderly widow with pretensions of tarot prescience, who tasked me to do her shopping and errands. She depended on me for grocery shopping and keeping her affairs in order, mostly utilities and medical bills. She was kind, kinder than I deserved perhaps. I doubted I could ever repay her generosity, and so I owed her as much as I could give as long as she was around. That kept me tethered in these moments. It would be cruel to leave her on her own. But once she was gone, then what would I do?

I imagined the body attached to the face on the overpass: slim hips, smooth skin, hands like a piano player's, skillful, fleet, cold, and hard-probing. Gripping my shoulder, they would pull me close in an urgent kiss like breathing air after years of drowning in muck. The tangle of our body parts would be irrevocable, staining each other with our fluid lust, moans from our lungs with the power and earthy resonance of bagpipes. From the pressure and heat, we would emerge as chimera, patchwork bodies in a patchwork town where nothing fit together neatly except the two of us, a two-piece puzzle set glued fast, tight, and complete.

I began to believe I might know whose face it was as memories swirled like chill wind through gaps in a house's framing. It was a fantasy, a lie; I knew that. Sometimes lies were the only food I could stomach. For not the first time, I was hostage to my unreasonable desires, and this one had no fix.

The face rose up again in mind, and I whispered the name aloud: "Luis." My desperate feelings and urges suddenly made sense. I'd felt this way in my high school days obsessing over Luis, a totally forgettable dude that I'd crushed on hard. We first became friends in band, third period, because we were the two new kids sophomore year. After winter break, my platonic feelings shifted. Fondness transformed to a primal hunger. I hid myself well, but as my ugly, stomach-churning, pitiful lust increased, it became harder for me to ignore that our relationship had changed, though he never said a word about it. Perhaps I was sneakier than I thought.

Months before I blurted my feelings to Luis, I had begun to notice the shape of his lips, to imagine my fingers in his hair, to hold myself back from pressing close in hugs because I wouldn't be able to let go. The self-seduction — my fantasy that this new arrangement was possible — was slowly persuasive and inevitable. I couldn't *not* believe my own argument, no matter how specious, and so it overtook me. Gradually. My silence was a breeding ground of self-deception. Stealthily, I was changed.

I came out to Luis in the most doom-fated way possible: instantly, hurriedly, insistently. His eyes widened in more than surprise. In horror. His conditioned heteronormativity was part of it. But he was more shocked by my betrayal. I'd destroyed our friendship by introducing a dangerous, foreign, and unfathomable element. The L word is anathema to a jaded teen, an utterance unacceptable to all but the most unconsciously normcore teens. We'd all learned in *Romeo and Juliet* that love unhinged.

I'd trapped myself; my words had tied knots nothing could unravel.

He revolted. I could not let go.

The feelings that tethered us together soured. The push-pull charge disgusted both of us before long. We didn't drift apart. We repelled.

I tried to put my memories of Luis aside. It couldn't be his face on the side of the freeway. I would have recognized him immediately. So why was I dredging up all this disgusting history?

I turned on my phone, blue glow lighting up the room, my finger hovering over the maps app, which displayed markers of several possible final destinations: desert, ocean, bridge, ravine, building. Then, instead, I conducted a search for the face with inadequate precision. The first few searches returned news stories of a rapper who stopped traffic both by looking like he might jump from an overpass and because he had an eight-pack of abs and pecs like two slabs of beef. Via Twitter, I found plans for housing developments on the few vacant lots left scattered through downtown and a list of macabre freeway deaths in L.A. County, topped by the man who was launched a hundred yards in the air and stuck to a sign above the 5. Macabre, I know. I fell asleep with the phone in my hand.

The next morning on my way to work, I resolved to get a photo of the picture. A pic of a pic. A perfect example of the derivative digital economy, though this was easier said than done. My windshield was pitted and never seemed to get clean, no matter how much Windex and scrubbing I applied. When I tried to stick my hand out the window and snap a pic, I couldn't get the angle right and the focus was off. One time I pulled to the side of the road where the 101 onramp met the 110, but the face wasn't visible. I needed to stop where there was no shoulder. Easy peasy.

In the middle of stacking books, while I felt feverish with sweat running down my back and swamping my pits, Alea came up, brow scrunched and frowning at her iPhone. On the back, plastic rubies and diamonds made a swirling pattern.

"You know Aunt Keema? Met her at the Rams party?"

"Mmm, nope. I don't think so." I'd been at her party for one sober hour of utter confusion and an unknown number of hours of inebriation and vomiting. A childhood shuttling back and forth between the East Coast and Ireland had prepared me well for West Coast debauchery: it wasn't my first blackout.

"Then how did she know you? Texted me with some bullshit."

She held the screen toward my face. I wiped my brow and reached for the phone to see better, but Alea held it back and gave me the stink eye. I squinted to read the message.

Tell your boy Deggan to watch out. Bad jujus. And then a string of inexplicable emojis.

I met her gaze solemnly. "Can I ask what exactly is a juju?"

Alea smirked and studied the message. "She thinks this some good gossip."

"What my people call *craic*."

She looked at me in warning. "Uh uh, don't say that here, you'll get your pretty teeth smashed and a whoopin' besides."

"Then you can call me 'gold grillz.'" I mugged a thuggish posture. "A proper look for a ghetto leprechaun."

She rolled her eyes and laughed, a layered sound both guttural and high-pitched, cavorting like music. Neither of us fit in with people we considered our people, so we could share these private jokes in a sanctuary full of learned tomes, ugly keychains, and private-labeled condoms. I knew better than to say such things on the street.

"So, how she know you my boy?" Alea asked.

"Fuck if I know. Does she have any advice for getting the jujus off me?"

"I'll ask." She typed out a message. The response came back right away.

Tell him to stop searching.

I gasped, feeling a burning coldness on the bottom of my feet like stepping onto snow without shoes.

"Don't worry. She cray cray. Spends it all on her organic tea and séances."

I laughed hollowly. Alea lifted an eyebrow but left me to resume stacking books. I had no idea where to pick up, so I took the pile back behind the counter and pretended to click through the inventory system for an hour, all the while trying very hard not to think about strange warnings from a crazy lady and, more importantly, why I couldn't heed her advice.

That afternoon on my way home, I found a side road that perched on a hillside overlooking the interchange. Although I couldn't see the face, I could study the landscape, the movement of the traffic, the way late-day light slanted into places that previously had been shadowed.

After the sun set and the landscape skewed toward a violet hue, I saw the perfect spot, a place where the 110 squeezed alongside an ivy-covered slope behind an apartment building on Sunset. It was nothing more than a wide part of the shoulder where the face could be visible to someone standing there, but it required hopping barbed wire surrounding the apartment complex wall or dashing across five lanes of traffic. I wouldn't try the stalled car trick again unless I had to, but maybe a smaller vehicle would do.

At work the next day, I asked Alea if she knew anyone with a scooter I could borrow.

"Vespa?" she asked.

"Sure."

"Nope. Vespas are gay."

"They're Italian."

"Italians are gay."

"Not gay enough. They've got the Vatican."

"Super gay."

I shook my head. "Not nearly enough, believe me."

"Try one of those electric ones. Lemon, or whatever."

"I want to take it on the freeway."

"Uh uh. Nope. You don't want to do that."

"I do."

"You'll get flattened. Smeared." She wrinkled her nose.

The next day, I downloaded an app and found an electric scooter lying on its side in front of the Central Library at the feet of a homeless man wearing a blue bandanna and with an American flag on a small stick poking from a basket on his wheelchair. He saw me looking and put a foot on the scooter. "Five bucks," he said.

"It's not yours," I replied.

"Not yours," he repeated, mimicking my voice in a high whine. Had I sounded that desperate?

I gave him five bucks, mentally making a note that I'd need to spend an extra half-hour at the bookstore and add it to my timesheet to make back the money. I was on a razor-thin budget. Every dollar counted. At least once a day I saw someone sipping from an obscenely large plastic cup full of sugar slurry and wondered how they could afford to spend that much money on getting diabetes.

The scooter bounced and lurched underneath my feet as it made a loop onto the freeway. I ignored the honks of drivers irritated that I could weave through slow-crawl traffic faster than they could, and more than a few astonished stares. They were penned in; I was free. The only threat was that a motorcycle would collide with me from behind, but I made it safely to the spot I'd picked out on the shoulder and looked up. There it was: the face. It wasn't Luis, and now I was sure it wasn't anyone I knew. Sad with longing, desperately disaffected, begging for connection. Maybe it was one of those composite images made by an artificial intelligence program that combined a thousand faces into one. Or maybe it was a face from history, someone who'd died before I was born.

For one confused moment, I thought it might be my own face. I feared maybe I'd come down with a rare disease — facial agnosia, also called face blindness. But when I snapped a selfie, I did recognize my own face, which was rounder, less emo, and more freckled, so that theory was debunked.

I took a dozen pictures, at various zoom levels and exposures, cursing myself for not bringing a real camera, for not taking any photography lessons, for being so clueless about one of the cornerstones of twentieth century art and the lifeblood of new new media. There was one photo, taken right before I bailed, that had the right focus, the right light balance to enact my plan.

Foolish me for thinking that taking a photo of something made it real.

Bartering sexual favors for professional services has never been easier thanks to the apps. I found a hung tech dweeb whose profile said he wanted to "give back to the community." He gave me a pounding, complete with a wobbly legged walk of shame, as well as access to an online facial recognition clearinghouse for what I told him was a "research project about policing and criminal justice." He didn't ask for more details, thankfully, and got me a login the same day. I uploaded the photograph, hoping for a match.

It returned nothing.

This was strange.

The clearinghouse tied into multiple databases. I knew for a fact that the prison system in California contributed their photos; it was a new way to keep track of probationers, and probably intended to intimidate them into behaving. But that was just a small portion of the potential pool of matches. The clearinghouse also tapped into Facebook, Twitter, Instagram, and every major dating site, even the religious ones. It really was cutting-edge with unprecedented and frankly scary access to millions of Americans faces.

And it didn't match a single one.

The next few days were a bit of a blur. I have memories of Alea yelling at me about Aunt Keema with my tinnitus drowning her out, but I can't remember why she was upset. The old woman I rented the house from was brought to tears by something I said, of which I have no recollection, other than a splay of tarot cards on her kitchen table. On my bank statement, I found a cash withdrawal for 60 dollars, plus fee, and I found an empty bottle of cannabis tincture in my bathroom trash. I also had trouble walking in a straight line, and my mouth felt like I'd bitten a fruit made of lava, permanently dry and painful. Thankfully, the student returned and took his car back, so that risk was gone too. Everything was a little bit fuzzy, and then gradually things returned to normal, if obsession and lunacy could ever be considered normal.

I borrowed a printer from the lab at school. They have no record of the agreement we came to unilaterally. A few days later, the printer snuck back in the night like a careless adulterer. I didn't think much of my impropriety: I needed the printer for my project, therefore I took it. I also borrowed several reams of paper.

The electric scooters I now used to get around town were the top-up pay-as-you-go kind. I swiped twenty dollars from my landlady's grocery change and bought a dozen rolls of tape and a staple gun. "Have you seen this face?" posters were now up in every street downtown, as far west as Koreatown and north to Griffith Park. I was working my way through Glendale and Highland Park, having already canvassed the Arts District, Boyle Heights, and half a dozen neighborhoods north of there.

The email address on the bottom of the poster received three or four messages a day. Most were queries asking which film marketing campaign these were attached to and whether I needed any freelance help. All of them were useless.

I updated my profile on Grindr to read, "looking for the floating face," and relevant details. The first useful message came through immediately, which should have freaked me out, but I was too elated to be concerned. The message from a blank profile said only, "I can help you. Call me," and gave a number.

I dialed, heart quickening, sure that I was about to be disappointed, but not able to wait more than ten minutes after the message rolled in.

"Hello?"

"Do you know who it is?" I asked.

"No. I don't know." The voice was soft, silky. "But I can help you find them."

"How?"

"Can we meet?"

"How can you help?"

"Have you heard of a summoning?"

I was half a breath away from hanging up.

The voice on the phone said, "The face wants to be found. You have to manifest your intention."

"What are you? A guru? A shaman? Why can't you tell me now?" I asked. My voice was angry, almost a shout, a thin veil separating outraged, eager, and out-of-control.

"I can help if you come in person." He dictated a place and a time, the next day.

When I showed up and knocked at the door of an apartment in East Hollywood, I was breathless, my insides churning. A long row of doors and slim walkways perched over parking stalls below, a deathtrap in an earthquake. My mind raced. I cursed aloud, but kept most of my monologue internal. Damn this shyster for giving me hope, curse him to a hell of saber-cocked buggery, and smash his balls in a pasta roller. My imagination was still riding the tincture high, apparently.

The door opened. His face was unremarkable enough that for a split second I wondered if his face was the one I was looking for. Then my vision came back into focus and

I realized his eyes were narrower, the nose more hooked, and the chin had a butt cleft that the floating face lacked.

"I'm Felix," he said.

"Deggan. How can you help?"

He ushered me inside. The gloom was only partially alleviated by faux-Edison-filament Christmas lights arranged in a circle and hanging from hooks on the ceiling, like a race track for fairies. The Tinkerbell kind. Alea would have been agog at the goth kitsch on the walls: black feathers, beads, glass fragments that I was sure were marketed as Satanist crystals. There was no couch nor any chairs in the living room, just pillows and small pedestals arranged to mark a circle the same circumference as the lights above. Below, on a four-foot diameter disk of black marble, proof this guy had access to gobs of cash from somewhere, was a pentagram made of salt.

"A proper portal to Hell," I said, not taking another step. Symbols written in glitter filled the interstices of the salt-shape. *Glitter*!

"A cleansed space," he replied patiently. He put a hand on my shoulder. "I'm not promising anything. You don't have to believe, but it would help. Wait here."

I obeyed, thinking that for all the out-of-touch, ivory tower babble among people I'd met at the university, we had at least shared a disdain of New Age crap. Yet here I was.

"I'm not giving you any of my blood."

"I don't do that," he said, this time sharply. He carried a painted wooden tray, smoothed to a black shine, and placed it at the center of the pentagon-in-pentagram. I sat across from him. He turned the crank on a small box and soon the room was buzzing with some sort of drone that probably had a story behind it that he was begging me to ask about.

"Have you seen the face?" I asked.

"Tell me about it."

"I don't know what I'm doing here."

"Describe it."

I sighed, my resistance ebbing. "The eyes are round, like they couldn't see enough of the world to shake off a loss or doom. Who is it?"

"Close your eyes and make a picture in your mind. Start with the face, only the face, nothing else, not the overpass, not the freeway, only the face. Everything else is black."

I listened and obeyed, trying not to think about the fact that I was sitting in a stranger's apartment that smelled of mold and had my eyes closed. I was at his mercy. I pictured a knife opening my throat. An axe in my skull. Hands stuffing feathers in my mouth until I choked. Knock it off, I told myself. Then the face loomed up as if illuminated by lights from below. A gulf of longing opened in the pit of my stomach. Why was I so tied to this image? Why couldn't I break free?

"You are connected to your vision," Felix said as naturally as if I'd spoken my questions aloud. "Your feelings are a reflection of the eternal truth present in every moment, every thought. We are all connected. The light of truth illuminates. The light surrounds the face. What do you see?"

I saw only the face, fragile, crystalline, suspended, alone. "Nothing, just the face."

"Look into the darkness. Are there shapes? Signs? Bring your light."

I opened my eyes. Felix stared at me. Eyes wide, bright white, reflecting what little light there was in the room.

"Why did you contact me?" I asked.

"You needed help," he said.

I looked at his face again. It held the broad, sincere, and utterly useless wonder of naïveté. He thought he was helping me. He was wasting my time.

"This isn't a spiritual quest," I said. "I'm looking for someone."

"What will you do if you find them?"

I held my breath. The fantasies of holding close, smelling skin, feeling safe and warm weren't something I was going to share with this stranger. "I don't plan to put a ring on it."

He didn't laugh. I didn't blame him.

I asked, "Can we keep trying?"

"I usually charge a fee," he mumbled. "For a summoning, it's 50 dollars."

I pressed my lips together, thinking about what meals I would skip, while we effectuated the payment with our phones.

"When you stop looking, things are found," he said.

"Fuck, this is hopeless," I muttered. I said things all the time without really thinking about them.

He looked at me long and strangely, cocking his head like confused puppy. He blinked three times rapidly. "You're right," he said, sounding surprised.

He jumped to his feet and walked past where I was sitting, wafting patchouli, body odor, and a sweet mixture of tobacco and cannabis. He ought to share his weed with me for what I was paying. He shuffled in the corner, dragged out a box from beneath a wax-encrusted coffee table, and searched through it. His labors scattered feather boas, sequined fabric, and bottles of glitter on the floor. I wondered if he knew of any good fancy dress parties I could be attending instead.

He turned back to me with a piece of lapis lazuli, a violet and navy mottled lump the size of a Ping-Pong ball, jagged, not at all manifesting the delicacy of a Goop catalogue item. He held it toward me. I began to reach, but he drew back his hand, not looking at me, gaze fixed on his rock.

Eventually, he met my eyes and looked at me like I was a street person approaching a stopped car at Hollywood and Vine, terrified, and said, "I can't help you."

"What?"

"I can't help you."

"I just paid you!"

"I'm sorry. We can do a refund. A partial refund."

"Why can't you help me?"

"It's not — I—"

"It's not you, it's me? Is that it?"

"You're in danger, Deggan."

I was livid. "I came here for help, not some sad riff on the Ghost movie."

"I can't help without —"

"Then what's the point of you! Oh, what? You want more money? Well, you can't, you took the last of it."

"Without putting myself in danger. I'm sorry. I can't."

"Well, Felix, my boy, you're a fucking wanker as they say. And I'll expect a refund."

I opened the door and escaped but failed to slam it as I'd intended, due to the screen door getting stuck open, and I wasn't going to be his freebie repairman, so I yelled "Feck off!" at the screen door and walked along the ledge of the apartment landing until I was on the sidewalk and then yelled a proper American "Fuck you!" — twice for good measure.

Fucking Felix.

It shamed me to have been cruel. I thought of apologizing, but he deserved my curses for wasting my time and asking for my money for a job not done. And neither of us got off.

When I told Alea at work the next day what had happened, she blamed me and laughed it off.

"Your fault for going in the first place. What did you think he was doing?"

"I don't know. I'm stuck, A. I'll admit I'm rightly fucked. There's a hole inside me and it hurts."

"Wow," she said, drawing out the sound and rolling her eyes. "That's so deep. Like buttfuls of ennui. I know! Maybe you could get a real problem to solve, like how we gonna get a raise before the holidays?"

"I'll pull myself together," I said, not really believing it.

A box arrived at work a week later with a sample T-shirt I'd ordered. "Have you seen me?" in bright yellow block letters layered on top of the grayscale face.

"What the fuck is that?" Alea asked.

"That's him. My ghost husband."

"He looks straight," she teased.

"Maybe I should have photoshopped him gay."

She traced a finger, this one now tipped by a red starfish on a blue background, across the curve of his lips and then cheek. "Needs some collagen. Trim the eyebrows. Maybe a nose ring?"

"Hot pink hair," I added.

The redesigned shirts arrived in less than two weeks. When people came into the store, usually it was for stationery or a coffee mug. We pushed the "missing person" shirts, adding a bit of lore. He'd been a USC student. He'd disappeared on his way back from frat party. No one at the school could remember meeting him. He was the disavowed.

I started a website called the Missing Trojan. There were some sly puns about unwanted pregnancies. Alea got some search engine optimization tips from a hot tech startup lady she knew (and regularly shagged). We started getting hundreds of hits per day, but unrelated junk continued to fill up my inbox. There didn't seem to be any good reason for it. My theory was that the bots were running the show already and we were just performing for their amusement.

Short on cash, I went on a few dates with some daddies. I ate well, enjoyed cocktails above my meager earnings, and put out once or twice, not very enjoyably — no one in L.A. likes it when you don't show the perfect blend of sufficient enthusiasm and epic chill, especially in bed — and I wondered which overpass I might jump off. It wouldn't seem right to do it where the face could see. But after thinking about it for far longer than was healthy, maybe my sacrifice would be worth it. Perhaps two ghosts were happier than one. Romeo and Juliet might have something to say about that.

At work, Alea showed me another message from Aunt Keema: *He's across the street. Watch out!*

Neither Alea nor I could muster the tiniest bit of humor for what I assumed was Aunt Keema trolling me. We both stared at it for a moment and then went about our business ignoring it.

My cleaning of the windows didn't last long. I put down the cleaner and the dirty rag I was using. The bell jangled as I left the bookshop. Alea didn't follow, though I wished she would. I was certain I wouldn't be able to say why I'd left, just as I was certain that I couldn't stop my feet from taking me toward the street.

Beyond the shelter of our building, a hot wind blasted me, almost knocked me over. Palm trees dropped jagged, heavy fronds on the sidewalk, scraping on concrete like nightmare devil brooms when gusts moved them. Walking was difficult, except when I turned in the direction of the intersection, and then the wind died down.

Nope. I didn't like that at all.

But when I reversed course, the wind kicked up dust that stung my eyes, dried my mouth, and made me cough. I turned again, the wind died again, and I stopped resisting, letting the sun roast me as I walked forward.

Traffic was backed up for three blocks due to construction that had dragged on for weeks. I threaded through standstill cars in the intersection, ignoring when drivers glanced my way, thinking about why they might continue to stare after catching a glimpse of me. I looked a wreck.

At the opposite corner, I spotted a tall black man in a mustard-yellow leisure suit. He seemed to be glowing, soaking up the day's heat and casting it outward, halo-like, in a way that made me think I might have been suffering from sunstroke.

Slowly, I approached where he stood on the corner. A wine-colored beret hid what I suspected was his complete baldness. He took off a pair of dark sunglasses and fiddled with them while he watched the opposite street corner as if expecting someone. Seeing his smooth skin and bright, wide-set eyes, I estimated his age at mid-twenties, though a hint of salt-and-pepper stubble betrayed his otherwise youthful glamour. (I later learned he was pushing 60.) His fake-Gucci leopard-print glasses held my attention. One arm of the glasses entered his mouth, and he sucked on it indelicately.

Minutes passed, then longer, and time seemed to thicken into a substance hard enough to carve notches in, like the rings on a nearby palm tree, notches of life reaching inward toward the end. And for what? If I were to mark every hour of my life, at the end, on my final day, would I rush to count them? Would the number ease my slipping away?

He finally looked down at me. His eyes widened.

I stood there, frozen, unable to speak. It wasn't that anything was stopping me; it was that the urge to do anything, anything at all — breathe, walk, turn, or scream — had literally left my body. My mind was paralyzed. I stood there stupidly for him to peer at. And slowly, mystifyingly, the aching need that had filled my chest for weeks began to subside.

"Speak, now that you're here!" he commanded in a voice deep with the ancestral power of taut, animal-skin drums.

With dawning realization, I said in a quiet whisper, "Oh my lord, I get it now. *You* were looking for *me*."

A strange thing happened: to answer him gave me pleasure. My boxers moistened with pre-cum. My heart hammered, both with lust and with the anger of a trapped animal.

"I'll admit you're not what I expected," he said in a slow drawl.

Hearing his disappointment, I became quite obnoxious in my desolation. "You're wearing a beret. I'm the one who's disappointed."

A cruel grin twisted his mouth. "Would you believe me if I said it was a magic beret?"

"I can't look away." My voice had faded to a tiny whisper. Tingling spread from my toes, followed by a floating numbness.

His grin grew wider. "Of course you can't."

And it was true. I stared, taking in his long-lashed eyes, broad shoulders, and a face that looked nothing like what I'd been searching for.

"Let's go back to something you said," he said. "*You're* disappointed? That's interesting. Must be the binding attunement."

I wanted to say I didn't know what the fuck he meant, but I was too busy wondering what he smelled like, what he looked like underneath his clothes.

After a moment, I managed to say, "You summoned me. Why?"

He smiled, self-satisfied. I tried not to stare at his soft, tender lips.

"I am Bertrand. You are mine now."

❧

In the weeks that followed, I grew accustomed to reading Bertrand's changeable moods and comporting myself accordingly. I'd never met someone with tempers so contingent on satisfying his appetites. No rage was more terrifying than a Bertrand who'd skipped a meal. No melancholy was more melancholic than when he felt I didn't demonstrate enough affection. His combination of psychological perception and otherworldly prowess overwhelmed me. He could snap his fingers and give me an erection. His fingers rubbing together when he was piqued felt like sandpaper burns from my head to my toes.

During long days of captivity my thoughts sloshed and swirled but never *stuck*. I lived from minute to minute in fear and despair with a few brief periods of respite when Bertrand used me in accordance with his will. I could form no plans for escape.

One night, with rain rattling the roof of a condemned house, we lay on a mattress in the middle of an unfurnished room surrounded by a circle of candles. He told me about the summoning, the many months of research and practice runs.

"Whose face was that?"

"Hmmm?" His arm held me close while his fingers caressed my nipple.

I levered myself up on an elbow and examined his face. "Why did you summon me with that face?"

He laughed. It shook the bed. His abdominal muscles evidenced supernatural origins — he hadn't been to a gym as long as I'd known him and yet he retained a strong, sleek, hard body that WeHo gym rats would kill for. I wondered if he'd ever killed anyone by his magic or by his powerful hands.

"Why did I think of Luis when I saw the face?" I demanded.

He kissed my forehead, and his lips' pressure sent a tingling through my extremities. Yes, my toes actually curled. "Who's Luis?" Soon, he rolled over and began to snore.

The candles guttered. In a house with no insulation, the wind blew through hidden cracks. I nestled against Bertrand's back for warmth, feeling the rise and fall of his breathing.

Later, sure that he was sleeping, I scooted to the edge of the bed, grabbed my phone, and called Alea. "You've got to get me out of here," I begged, whispering.

"Keema says you've got a sugar daddy now," she told me, squealing delightedly. I thumbed the volume to its lowest setting. "Are you ever coming back to work?"

"You have to get me out of here. I'm a slave," I hissed.

"Don't pull that shit with me," she snapped. In a gentler tone she went on, "Look, swirling's not easy. You're both coming from different worlds. You have to work at it."

Bertrand's snores sounded like an overpowered leaf blower. I pressed the phone to my ear until it ached. "Please, Alea, I can't stop myself. I'm powerless."

Eventually, after I whispered through the phone for a half hour, she came to understand, with appropriate levels of dismay and remorse, the nature of my situation. She conference-called Aunt Keema, who stopped me halfway through my detailed explanation of my ongoing defilement and said every bigwig of the arcane L.A. underground knew about my ensnarement. She agreed to help — when she could. She had to wait for a change in the moon-Jupiter aspect, something to do with Other Side harmonics. I didn't quite follow.

In the morning, I begged Bertrand to explain what was happening. I said I needed to understand my situation to be content with it. In reality, I hoped he'd let spill some weakness I could use to break the spell.

He took me to a vacant building on Temple Street, a three-story office building from the fifties that looked like an earthquake deathtrap. Pushing aside a plywood barrier at the front door, we squeezed inside and found a dimly lit expanse of concrete covered with trash and excrement. A stairwell in the corner led up to the third floor where a breeze cleaned out the stench from below. At a hole where a window had once been, Bertrand pointed southeast. The freeway overpass was visible. There was no face.

"You saw a shadow of what you needed. Thousands of people passed by every day and didn't see a thing. You're special. There was no face there for anyone but you."

"Luis?" I asked.

He waved a hand in dismissal. "A memory. A figment. Your mind calling up associations to fulfill the needs of my spell, my wish."

I thought about visiting Felix; he'd known something wasn't right. I wished I'd taken his fear to heart. Maybe if I saw him again, he could help me break out or maybe we could shag. In any case, I tried to imagine other ways to test the boundaries that Bertrand had set for me. And secretly, I hoped that one day Aunt Keema would come through for me.

Bertrand faced me, pulled me close in a deep kiss, then turned so we could watch the traffic together. Pairs of brake lights flashed red below the concrete bridge. L.A.'s towers glinted in smog-tinted light. I breathed deep and smelled exhaust with a faint trace of jasmine, probably a wild vine, nourished in a crack of the barren patchwork streetscape.

I glanced at Bertrand. He was content for the moment. I wondered though what would happen when he was done with me. I had nothing to go back to, nothing of my own. But I couldn't remain ensnared. Not for much longer anyway.

TWO KINGS

C. Gregory Thompson

A body falls out of the sky, landing on the hood of my car with a metal-crunching thud. Whites of eyes, brights of teeth. Brakes screech, fast glances in the rearview hoping there's no one behind to slam into me. I turn Marilyn Manson's shrieking "Born Villain" off as the Ford LTD lurches to a stop on the shoulder. A mound of flesh lies outside the windshield, still, unmoving. Not sure if dead or alive. Blood smears, trickles, across the cracked safety glass. Arms twist in unnatural directions. Face looking in at me. Cold, staring eyes. This isn't happening. Stomach, guts roil, nausea. Sweat prickles across the top of my head. I open the driver's side door and throw up. I can't be found with a dead body. Cannot. Can't stay here, can't be seen. What the fuck do I do? Shit. Think, Brett, think. I put the car in gear and carefully pull back onto the ten-lane concrete freeway.

The 210 between Tujunga and Pasadena is empty at three in the morning on a Tuesday in January. I head to the closest exit, Pennsylvania Avenue. A quarter-mile away. I pray no one else drives this stretch. Or sees us. The body, a man with a full beard, brown skin, black hair, wearing paint-spattered jeans, dirty white Reebok tennis shoes, and a Dodgers windbreaker, wobbles slightly as the car jostles side to side. The man's curls blow around in the freeway speed-induced wind. Who is he? Did he jump? Fall? Why the hell me? He still stares. The eyes saying, "Help me."

The police? Not an option. A hospital? Can't happen. Fuck, I can't do this right now. I just picked up several pounds of shit. $50K worth. From a guy who cooks in Tujunga. Tomorrow's market day. My regulars know Wednesday's their day. Why me now? I take the Pennsylvania Avenue exit, go up the off ramp, and find a residential street. I know the area well. I make my pickups late at night because no one's ever out. I drive along. Houses, dark, one after the other, blur by. Hiding on small streets, away from commercial thoroughfares, possible sightings, and peering security cameras. I pull into Crescenta Valley Park and stop under the oak trees. Gnarled branches, leaves a deep green, wild and overgrown, hover over and protect me from view. When I turn off the engine, it sputters before going quiet. I sit, looking forward, at the bearded face, blood dribbling from a corner of the limp mouth, between purplish lips. The eyes continue their help-me stare.

Selling meth wasn't part of the plan when I started as an English major at UC Santa Barbara. Sophomore year I met a girl who dealt drugs. All kinds. She could get anything. I learned from her. We started fucking. Fun fucking. No agenda for bigger things. She liked the way I felt, and I liked the way she did. In sync. She taught me *not* to be an addict. A sample now and again to check the quality, but no regular using. She'd say, "It's a business. You have a product they want. Success requires staying clean." When she graduated, I took over her practice. When I graduated with honors, I didn't stop dealing. I never knew why. I haven't spent time trying to figure it out. Probably for a list of mundane reasons. Laziness, it was so easy. Lucrative, I made a shit-load of money. Tax-free dollars, too. Renegade, not a fan of the status quo, I could remain a rebel into adulthood. It became my profession: Drug Dealer. Now, at age thirty-one I wouldn't say I'm proud of it, nor humbled by it. I've handled everything it threw at me until now.

I open the car door, the oil-needing creak startling me, and put a tan-colored Carthartt work boot on the pavement. The Santa Ana winds blow cold. Branches on the oak trees rustle violently, leaves and dust float in the air. Grabbing the doorframe, I pull myself out of the car. Three steps forward and I can touch the man. News of a slow pulse doesn't solve a thing for me. Dead instead of alive might have been easier. Either way, *I'm still screwed.* Decision-time forces me back behind the wheel. We can't hang out in the park. Moving him into the car will take too long. Better he stays in position. Returning to the residential side streets, I drive us home. To my place, a dump of a house I rent in the foothills of La Crescenta, a place that's off and away from others. A short, densely tree-lined driveway leads back to a half-acre plot with a two-bedroom house. The house needs everything done to it a house could need. I don't bother harassing the landlord to make the repairs. I pay my rent six months at a time, and he leaves me alone. He likes the cash.

Did the dude fall? Did someone push him? Questions flood my brain. Who is this person? Where are his people? He comes from someone, somewhere out there. He has a mother and father. Is there a wife? Are there children? Are there hearts loving him, needing him, wanting him? Life's shitty to some of us. His brown skin in Southern California makes him in all probability Latino. Illegal? Maybe here alone with family back in Mexico, or some other Central or South American country. Paint on his pants, I bet he's an under-the-table housepainter, making crap money, paying off his *coyote* and wiring the rest home to his family. Sad and shitty. Did he fall trying to get away from somebody? A thug the *coyote* sent to collect his overdue debt? Pesos on credit spent with a prayer that a better life awaits. Or maybe he was pushed over by the husband of the woman he took up with? A woman he knew from his village back home. He jumped because the prayer went unanswered. The better life never arrived. He knew he would be paying the *coyote* back forever. He jumped because the woman, the girl-love from his childhood, decided to stay with her husband.

I sit in the LTD in front of my house, hands fused to the steering wheel, ten and two o'clock, turning white from gripping too tightly. I know I need help, but who? Pushing synapses to make electrical connections. I reach Hank — a client, a meth head, yes, but an ex-EMT if I remember correctly — on my cell phone, and he agrees to come over. When he arrives, he immediately goes hardcore EMT, tossing out phrases like triage, blood loss, amputation. I know it's the meth talking. I calm him down, and he does a quick assessment of the man before we move him. He still lives; the slow pulse shows a heart pumping enough blood to keep him breathing. I've grown used to the unblinking, staring eyes, to the mangled, bloody, inert body. We carefully move him off the LTD's hood onto a plastic tarp I keep in the trunk. Inside we place him on the bed in the spare bedroom. A room where I dump crap I can't deal with. Tall stacks of cardboard boxes full of books, magazines, and old news-papers tight up against the walls make it hard to navigate. Hank squeezes in and checks him over with a razor-sharp attentiveness borne of his addiction. I watch and wait. Confirmed alive, not yet dead. What does that mean now? What will happen to him? What will happen to me? Questions, thoughts, fragments of energy continue to ping-pong inside my cerebral cortex. Adrenaline my drug, not meth.

I search his pockets to see if he has a name, something to tell me who he is in this world. Who his mother and father wished him to be: a Pedro, a Miguel, a Jesus, or a Javier? Inside a worn-out leather wallet I pull out of his back pocket are two twenty-dollar bills and a photo of a woman holding a young girl. Something's written on the back in Spanish I'm unable to read. No driver's license or government-issued identification. Death suddenly complicates life. If he dies, I won't know who he is, I won't be able to return his body to those who love him, or tell them of his passing. I'll have to dispose of him, his corpse. The empty shell he leaves behind. Toss him on the side of the road like he's a victim of a hit and run? Too risky. Easy to be seen, caught. Take him to the desert and put him in a shallow grave? The type animals dig up, exposing a long-unsolved crime. A jawline appears, gold tooth glinting in the desert sunshine. Sheriff's deputies, detectives, and forensic specialists with their cameras, tools, and brushes descend and excavate the rest of the skeletal remains. Best for me if he stays alive. Best for him? I can't answer. For now, he'll be a Juan Doe instead of a Pedro, a Miguel, a Jesus, or a Javier.

I help remove his dirty, bloody clothes and watch as Hank methodically starts to repair the most obvious injuries. I clean dried blood off the man's hands and face. I look into his still open eyes and answer the questions they ask. Yes, I'm going to help you. Yes, I'll try to keep you alive. Hank wants to take him to a hospital. I tell him no, that's not possible. If we do, they'll ask questions, they'll report it. An investigation would bring cops to my door. I could go to prison, and my business would close. Hank agrees to treat him there, in my house. He has me write out a list of things he needs, and I leave to get them. With the items I bring back, and with stolen EMT supplies he already has, Hank makes casts for two legs and one arm; sutures cuts on the man's face, chest, and legs; bandages open wounds; and starts an IV drip. The spare room emerges from its normal squalor and morphs into a quasi-hospital room.

Hank stays with us. I ask him to, I need him to. Without X-rays and a hospital, we don't know if the man has internal injuries. Time will provide the answer. Meth-addled Hank makes the man his project. He likes putting his EMT experience to use. I pay Hank in meth. He binges when he needs to but still maintains enough to care for his patient.

A week passes and the man comes to, wakes up. His eyes blink rapidly. He squints at the bright overhead light, groans at the pain he abruptly feels, and mumbles in Spanish. He tries to get up, to move, to leave. Hank and I hold him down. I tell him he must stay still. I ask his name. No response. He looks at us with fear in his eyes.

"English? Do you speak English?"

"A little," he answers.

⊘

Santa Anas, that's what they call them. Devil winds. *El viento del diablo.* Salvador learns of them when he's first in *el Norte.* Fiercely they blow, hot sometimes, others cold. They piss off men and frighten children. The mountain passes, the canyons give them life. They shrill down at more than forty miles an hour, tossing palm tree fronds into the streets, stirring up dust and grit, and making the people of Los Angeles act crazy. L.A., Salvador's new city. The name's so pretty in Spanish, it reminds him of Mexico, of home. *El Pueblo de Nuestra Señora la Reina de Los Angeles.* The Town of Our Lady the Queen of Angels. Little towns all over Mexico are named after the Virgin too.

Devil winds, cold, make his eyes water, and chap his skin on a Tuesday night in January. End of a day, his last on a job painting a house in a place he doesn't know. La Crescenta, a town near mountains he can see from the flats below. A two-hour bus ride, up, from the single room he shares with seven men, all like him, in downtown "El Lay." A room the landlord kicks them out of that morning. Where will he sleep tonight? Forty dollars, all he makes for two days' work. The only job he has all month. When he doesn't work, he puts his hand out. Walking in traffic on Alvarado Street, holding a cardboard sign with something written in black marker. He recognizes the word "hungry," *hambre* in Spanish. A sign he finds in the gutter that another *pobre* like him leaves behind. Strangers rarely help. A dime, a quarter, a one-dollar bill. Not enough. The burning, gnawing in his stomach never leaves. Three meals a week is about all he eats.

Homeless, he walks for hours. Where's he to go? Walking across a bridge that spans a freeway, he stops in the middle. He climbs. Up the chain link fence, a protective barrier to the concrete roadway below. At the top, he stops and looks down at the rushing-by cars. He's Salvador, his grandfather's name, his mother's father. Twenty-nine years ago his *mamá* gave birth to him in their town, Dos Reyes, "Two Kings," located in the state of Jalisco. Last year, in December, he paid a *coyote* to smuggle him across the Rio Grande into the US. No jobs in Dos Reyes. No money to support his wife and little girl. Not a man. A man takes care of his family. A family he probably won't see again. Three-thousand dollars, his debt to the *coyote*. Money he doesn't have. Dollars he won't ever possess.

He jumps. Up. Into the night sky. He's flying. Freedom. The air, icy, burns his skin, seeps beneath the windbreaker he wears. Then, he feels nothing. Unafraid, he's not there. Gone, into the ether of time. Nonexistent, soul fleeing earthly confines. Plasma, tissue, bones, blood lacking form, void of humanness. Now he knows everything. He returns to his physical body, a split second only, when it hits something hard, metal, warm, roaring and moving faster than the devil winds. The hurt doesn't last. The pain, the ache of broken bones departs quickly. Angel-like, he soars back up, rapidly. Out of body, to that happiness he never knew until now. Wants to remain there. He looks down on his mangled body, lying on the hood of a car speeding down a freeway he doesn't know in *el Norte*. He wonders: what's happening? What did I do? Am I dead? No, still alive, pain of his broken body a distant ebbing echo. The car stops, fast, jerking him forward. He almost falls off, but the dent made by his body hitting the car's hood holds him in place. He lays twisted and torn, the iron and steel protecting him. An orange light blinks on and off, on and off, on and off, and the car slowly moves back onto the freeway. Where's he going now?

A funerary chariot, the car slinks along neighborhood streets, slow and fast, abrupt turns and sudden stops. Is the driver escaping? His body jostles back and forth, side to side, in time to the swaying movements of the rumbling machine. Who's driving? His eyes, wide open, looking for knowledge, for answers. His two legs and one arm hurting so damn much, cracked, broken from the velocity of his two-hundred plus pounds slamming into the metal of the car. Blood trickling from open wounds, drying in the rush of air. He's un-whole, shattered, at the edge. An open door, ethereal figures beckon to him. They call to him in Spanish, asking him to join them, to go with them. Where're we going? He starts to follow. They're his long-dead *abuelos*, his grandparents. They say to him, "Come, *ven mijo. Ven!*" Trees, shadows, the winds, a tall white man who touches his neck, then darkness. He no longer sees his body. He leaves it, now a heap of flesh on the hood of the car. He floats off, above, away.

"Salvador!" His mother calls to him. He's five, and they are at his grandfather's farm in Jalisco. He's in a field with the animals: the sheep, the cows, the goats, and the chickens. Running, playing with his cousins, he's King of the Hill. They have wooden swords. They fight each other off a dirt mound to be the supreme ruler of all the land.

"Salvador!"

"One more minute, *mamá*! I'm King of the Hill." He tells his cousins to obey his commands, or they will be sent to the dungeons and held prisoner.

"We're leaving now, Salvador. Come, please. Be a good, sweet boy for your *mamá*."

He shouts back to her, "I'm coming *mamá*!" He enters a vortex, winding around and around. He runs up the dirt mound, back down and up again, over and over, repeatedly. He doesn't mind. Time ceases. He runs up and back down, up and back down. Up and back down.

He hears himself speaking foreign words. "A little," he says. Who's he talking to? His eyes flutter fast, but he doesn't see, a blur. A room somewhere. He lies in bed. Bright light overhead. The room smells damp and musty. Shadows move over him. Someone's speaking to him in English. His body hurts the most unbearable pain.

⟨⟩

Seven days after Salvador tried to kill himself by jumping off a freeway overpass, he woke up. Relieved he hadn't died, my first thought then was, "What now?" I saved the man, but what do I do with him now? He wasn't well enough to leave, but eventually he'd have to. Over the next several weeks, he steadily improved. Once he was able to get out of bed, he moved around, awkwardly with the two leg casts. I helped him at first. He slowly ventured into other parts of the house: the living room, the kitchen, the bathroom. We ate meals together usually with the television on, little to no conversation. Salvador sat in an old, stained armchair in the living room, TV remote in his lap, watching *fútbol*. He surfed the Spanish stations, watching as much of Mexico's national team as possible. Soccer wasn't a sport I knew much about. I sat and watched with him, learning about this passion of his. Weak, nodding off, his strength not fully recovered, I'd highjack the remote and switch the channel to COPS. He'd wake up and say, "*Ay, no!*" He hated that show, he said in a mix of Spanish and English, it made him nervous, the police chasing after criminals and arresting them. An impasse, eventually achieved: he watched soccer when his team played; asleep, he snored loudly, his objection, when I watched COPS.

Just like roommates. My first since college. Alone, my preference, a life routine interrupted, forced upon me. By week six, the wariness I felt from him since his arrival disappeared. An exuberance emerged, his energy returned, I experienced him as he probably would be at home, in Mexico with his family. He spoke to me in Spanish despite my not understanding, teasing me, mocking. I could tell by the inflections and the occasional *hijo de puta* and *cabron*. I tossed it right back at him in English he didn't understand. I frightened myself when I realized I liked having him around, semi-mended. A rapport with another person I'd not known I was missing. *Hermanos* maybe?

I continued operating my business. Wednesday was still the busiest day of the week — with clients coming and going all day, not easy to hide. I figured if Salvador had issues with it, he could leave. He wouldn't go to the police since he wasn't legal. Besides, we trusted each other. Not only *hermanos* but *muy buenos amigos*. I had so few really good friends.

Three months in, Hank removed the casts from Salvador's arm and legs. The bone in one of his legs hadn't knitted together properly. He now walked with a limp. I felt such sorrow for him. A brotherly *oh, fuck, no*. One more thing to add to the difficulties of his life. Difficulties I didn't possess. Why him and not me? Why some people and not others? Inequities of our existences I'd never understand. When he stepped now, his right leg swung out from his hip and down. A hitching, halting gait, now the first thing people would notice. Before his brown skin, before his accent.

The day Hank removed his casts, Salvador offered to work for me. My first reaction was no, no way. I can't work with someone else, not a stranger. But business had been good, and I saw this as a way for Salvador to earn the money he'd need to leave. I wasn't sure if I wanted him to go. The place would be empty without him. I probably feared living my solo life again. Not sure why, on gut instinct only, I liked and trusted him. For three months, I'd watched the man, studied him, and learned about him. A risk, yes, but one I decided to take.

☽

On his first awake Wednesday, Salvador looked out the bedroom window — he heard noises. All day long people came and went, parking their cars, knocking lightly on the front door, and leaving a few moments later. He wondered if Brett was selling drugs. *Hielo*? Ice? Yes, probably. If this *gabacho*, this white boy, sold drugs, that was his business. He momentarily wondered if the meth Brett sold came from the cartel near his village. He spent most of his time missing his family — his wife, Maria, and his little girl, Angela. Watching TV in a bathrobe Brett gave him, too small and smelling like the white boy, Salvador kept the only photo he had of his wife and little girl in one of the robe's two pockets. He touched the pocket often or pulled the picture out to hold. When Brett wasn't in the room, he spoke to the image. Telling them how much he missed them, how he wished he could come home soon. He wiped away tears with a bathrobe sleeve if Brett appeared.

Salvador, stuck in place, beholden to the white boy, trapped by weakness, worried about what he would do once he was well enough to leave. Here, he had everything he needed. Should he try to stay? Would Brett let him? Or should he try, again, to find work as a *pinche mojado*, a fucking wetback.

Pretending to like the stranger caring for him exhausted him. He wanted to watch *fútbol* alone without the white boy asking questions he couldn't answer. He wished he could stand so he could cook a meal, a *puchero*, a nice beef stew, from back home. One of the dishes his mother made. Enough with the hot dogs, cans of soup, and take-out pizza Brett fed him. His face hurt from smiling, pretending to understand the white boy's jokes, pretending they were friends when he believed they weren't. Strangers, passing acquaintances only.

A knock on the door one afternoon when Brett was out. Not the normal day for sales. Pounding woke Salvador up. He hobbled to the front door and opened it. A young woman, messy red hair, scabs on her arms and legs, teeth yellow and rotting, stood looking in at Salvador. Not a regular customer.

"Please? A friend told me I could score here."

Salvador told her *no inglés*, but he knew why she was there. She held cash out to him, eighty dollars. He told her he couldn't, in Spanish, over and over while closing the door. She pushed it open.

"Por favor."

He knew how much to give her. If Brett thought Salvador was asleep, he'd work in front of him, so Salvador learned to sleep with an eye open. He grabbed a half-gram from Brett's stash, inside a banged-up, putty-colored, metal file cabinet in the living room, took the girl's money, and she left. Then, he slowly worked his way across the living room, holding on to pieces of furniture, and slid the cash underneath the mattress in his room. Before hiding the money, he kissed it and prayed a novena to St. Jude, patron saint for those in need. During Salvador's twelfth week of healing, the other white boy, loco Hank, removed the casts from his arm and legs. Up and walking around, and feeling much better, he asked Brett if he could work for him.

The sixth night of Salvador's career as a drug dealer was a Tuesday, the day Brett always picked up his supply of *drogas*. Brett drove the LTD as they went to a place called Tujunga. Another town Salvador didn't know in *el Norte*. He sat in the passenger seat looking out at the dent his body had made in the car's hood. It was the middle of the night when they made the run. The devil winds blew again but this time warm, not cold. Windows open, hot gusts pushed through the car. He closed his eyes, the rocking sensation of the machine lulling him into a half-sleep. On the return trip, eighty miles an hour on the 210 east, a week's supply of meth secure in the trunk, the overpass appeared above them.

He remembered. Climbing up the protective chain-link fence, pausing at the top, falling forward, jumping, and slamming hard into warm metal, then nothing. Brett looked over at him when they went under the overpass. Salvador didn't look back. He sank lower into the car seat, turned his face into the rushing wind, and closed his eyes. Dozing, warm air soothing, he heard his mother call: "Salvador! We're leaving now. Come, please. Be a good, sweet boy for your *mamá*."

That night, late, alone in his room, he knelt, elbows on the bed, hands together in prayer. He prayed to *la Virgen*, the blessed Virgin Mary. He prayed for forgiveness, for sins he'd already committed and for future sins he might make. He asked her to come to him. To remain at his side. To walk with him as she had before. He remained on his knees, mumbling in prayer, for over an hour. When he felt God's grace within him again, he went to Brett's stash and grabbed up all that was there. Next he went to where Brett hid his cash, a ceiling panel above the refrigerator. He reached in and removed it all, just over fifteen thousand dollars. He put the drugs and the money into a duffel bag, and then he quietly opened the front door and walked, his halting, hitched, one-two gait, away, into the night. Down the driveway, to the street, along the neighborhood block, to the boulevard at the bottom of the hill, on his way home.

MOUTH BAY

Nolan Knight

As a child, my dreams were infinite as sunray glitter across Santa Monica Bay. I can see them all now, a legion of sparkles ignited then killed, out past the break. One flashes gymnastic glory: eight years old: summer Olympics fever. Another glimmers horseback rides through Palos Verdes bridle paths, age ten. But all those dreams died when I hit thirteen, as if stray kelp shackled my ankles, dragging me beneath crashing waves. *Was it really* love *when it came to that boy?* Then Missy: six pounds, eight ounces — nineteen inches long. I sank like a moon rock: cool, hard, weightless. That's about it for this pretty bitch — trapped in coral for so long, have to check my damn throat for gills …

"You okay there, Randi?"

Wet hands drop from my neck. "What?"

The goatee bounces. "Everythin' alright?"

I shut off the running faucet, drying with a busser's rag atop a mound of crusted forks. "Yeah … Just thinkin', Sal."

"Great … Hey, can you finish those thoughts on break? We're gettin' slammed in the ass out there."

I peer over his shoulder through crooked saloon doors. Place doesn't seem rowdy for a Friday dinner rush. Other waitresses are slouched over the bar, gazing back as if I am another rat in the kitchen. Their star-spangled bikinis clash with faux-leather chaps; hard faces masked by seven-layer dip. I swipe a mock Stetson from off a chopping block. "Sure thing — lemme just grab these hot wings for table nine. Be right out."

❧

Wafting wing sauce burns the eyes. I saunter through tipsy old men over to a family near the John Wayne mural. Dad ogles my implants; Mom kisses her infant's hand to earn a cackle. When Missy was that tiny — couldn't remember ever taking her into restaurants. Now she's nine; rather dive into her *Goosebumps* than sit at a table in public with me. Not sure if she's embarrassed or simply going through pre-pubescent weirdness — either way, she'll have to deal with me, same as I did her. Can't blame her. I mean, neither of us asked for this.

I sidle up to the bar, pretending to search for a customer's check. Sal is out smoking another Parliament with the new teenage hostess. I can tell she'll be in flip-flops her whole life. Beach's tractor beam takes hold of most around here. Willy gets a drink from the bartender, slides the double of Grey Goose into my hand and smacks the rose on my right butt cheek.

"Howdy, Mama."

I feign a smile, tossing a candy cane straw into the glass.

He's an old crooner, grumbling slow ballads on a stool under the big screen most nights. How he thinks he can compete with the Lakers, I'll never ask. Sings for drinks and never takes requests; by the smell of his breath, tonight began with a bang. Drives one of those custom Econolines — I caught him in a Vons parking lot once, loading his invalid wife into its rear. Tubes in her frozen face, feet gnarled as bitten taffy. Never told him about it though. Couldn't wreck his fantasy. This dump: only place he can put on for others.

I crunch an ice chip, placing a cold kiss to his brow. Janelle (the blue-haired barkeep) snaps a towel at me.

"Better get on, Rock Star. Dora's over there clearing your table."

I make a kissy face and hit the floor.

Rock Star: a blatant dig into my past. I've been called worse. When I made it with Hank Raskin by the Wilderness Park swamp, everyone began to call me "In-N-Out." That lasted through middle school — till I met Tommy. We'd shared a joint at a Rat Beach bonfire. Everyone questioned his choice; told him of my tales, now taller than the downtown skyline. He blew 'em off — became my shield. The lead singer of Smarm. Newest band in the South Bay with a record deal. Surf punk. Members were all of seventeen. Songs about shattered homes, bones, and relationships (best they knew). Backyards and basements brought notoriety. Fast-living fueled egos. How was a girl not supposed to get trapped in that riptide?

Wild years slugged along. I grew entitled: backstage at every Hollywood venue, canoodling with icons, free drinks, good drugs. The title of Tommy's girlfriend was most intoxicating. I'd been faithful; too scared to ask him flat out. Not like I'd leave. Once Smarm toured Europe a third time, distance brought disaster. He was in Munich when I told him the doctor's prognosis to my sudden nausea spells. Three months in, six to go. His silence still brings chills.

The marriage lasted till Missy was two — eighteen months of which Tommy was somewhere on a bus through America. Interviews with various rock rags never came close to who he really was. I felt duped. Soon after the divorce, couldn't remember who I was anymore. Time had erased all those swells of future's promise. I live in a world where an embellished reputation defines me to others. *They don't call the South Bay* "Mouth Bay" *for nothing.* Twenty-six years on the run …

Have I ever been anything more than lowbrow gossip?

@

My shift ends. Soon as I hit the parking lot, some fucker who'd been swilling Beam near the popcorn machine tries to walk me to my car. I pretend I'm not feeling well, and he sneers in rejection. Truth is, I've felt lousy all day: stomachache/backache/headache. I'm going through the motions — no longer life's participant. *Hopefully not coming down with something sinister.* Prolly need more meds.

The Cabriolet is finally paid for. Got the pink slip and everything. Cutest car *ever*. Seven long years, and I'm the proud owner of an eighteen-year-old convertible that needs new brakes. My lone accomplishment, thus far — even though my folks *did* place the down payment. A gift for getting my G.E.D. (I cheated.) My purse rattles a pill vial tune. The sound always reminds me of those cartoon skeletons — hammering each other's dry bones like xylophones. They started me off with one vial for anxiety; ten years later, I'm basically a pharmaceutical rep. They're good to have on hand, but I've never really needed 'em. Made up most my symptoms in the beginning: a foot in the door with doctors. That's the best way to land cures for pain.

I crush a Vicodin ES with my cherry lip gloss; spread it along the dash with Mom's Nordstrom card. A post-shift ritual: that Marlboro after rough sex. I gauge for nostril dregs in the rearview. (Dad mentioned something, few days back.) Blood neon catches my eye: *Texas Loosey* is awash down my rear plastic window.

Key turns.
Clutch sticks.
One more try, and I win.

☉

My folks took us in when they evicted me from the Sea
Breeze. Mom doesn't mind Missy; Dad calls me "The
Squatter." I can still unlock the front door without clacking the bolt; any magician will tell you that a high-caliber
illusion (such as this) is only perfected over a thousand
grand performances. Imagine what I can do after a million. Missy and I share what used to be Dad's den. Whenever my trick goes bust, she'll stir and moan, eventually
cursing me for brushing my teeth with the light on. I'd
ask her to come with me to the beach tomorrow, before
my afternoon shift, but I'm sure she won't. Last time she
wore Dr. Martens and draped herself in black denim while
I baked evenly in the sun. I swear if it wasn't for *me,* we'd
get pegged as outsiders — sand poachers from Hawthorne
or Lomita. Hey, I didn't suffer the torments of this place to
be anything but a local! Christ. One day Missy'll fucking
get it.

My stomach howls. I haven't eaten anything but yogurt
today. Mom's reading something romantic at the kitchen
table, sipping her chamomile tea. She stopped coloring her
hair last year for some reason. Wisps of grey streak here
and there; the mother who raised me wouldn't have left
the house in curlers. I hope one day I too can let go — get
lost in some trashy love realm made up of greased abs and
veiny biceps. I'm careful not to make a peep, knowing how
Mom gets when she's immersed. Her eyes scan a page as if
I'm some specter passing through. I dig at a familiar itch
on my nose. She knows I'm out of it but doesn't harp.

Gave up on me after the last rehab — told me I was merely a headstone in this family. Pretty sure she turned to the dark side after I got caught breaking into houses, pawning any score for pills or worse. *My little illusion can open most doors.* Needless to say, police station/jail visits wear on parents. I don't blame her. She slurps a gulp and says to me, "We ate Ruby's earlier — no leftovers. Haven't gone shopping either."

I put a little sugar in my voice. "'Kay, Mom." A jar of pickles waves at me when I open the fridge.

"Missy needs new reading glasses, you know?"

My eyelids fall. "'Kay."

"The pair she liked was a hundred twenty."

"Well, I get paid next week, so …"

"Oh, I already bought them for her. I'm telling you how much you owe us."

I close the refrigerator gently and head back to the den, crunching into the pickle as if it were a live pigeon.

۵

Can't remember a summer in Redondo ever being this humid. Thick, sticky — like breathing through a crazy straw. Zero waves, longboarders speckling the coast in denial. Beachgoers remind me of ants on a hill. Good thing I can still kill a bikini. I'm tan all year for this reason alone. Missy didn't want to come with me, so I called up my one girlfriend (Donna). I don't have to be at work till four. We're meeting on the pier for daiquiris and a man hunt. Haven't seen anyone in weeks that gets us wet, but we love talking shit, damn good at it too.

My roller skates were once pristine: creamy suede, bubblegum pink wheels. That was when Tommy got 'em for me one Christmas, twelve years ago. Prolly shouldn't wear them anymore, but I can't afford a new pair (thanks to Missy). They have more mileage than the Cabriolet, easily. Everyone I know who rides skates has broken their tailbone at least once. Not this girl. It's a simple glide that I've perfected over the years, nearly effortless on The Strand's sleek concrete. I am grace incarnate upon spinning polyurethane, swinging my arms with a fluidity that swishes my glistening bust for all to see. Dudes must think I was a professional ice skater at one time — an athlete — someone important. I pretend like I don't notice their stares, but I see 'em, love 'em — slurp 'em up for breakfast!

☯

Barney's Beanery is the newest haunt on the second tier of the Redondo Pier. I used to go to the original in West Hollywood whenever Tommy played the Troubadour. Be surprised if this one lasts longer than the previous pub. Doesn't matter. Some other lush den will take its place. All it takes is for locals to turn their backs (which is a given), and then I have a peaceful hangout till the place files for bankruptcy.

I sling my skates over a shoulder and hit the patio. Donna is giggling in a booth, fluffing a waiter barely out his teens. Behind her, the Pacific is cold and tepid. She's my best friend, but I couldn't tell you her exact age or what neighborhood she grew up in. An army brat from Vegas, I think. Used to work Loosey's with me before they caught her skimming tips. She's nearly twice my size (in weight not height). Used to be a double threat, but last year she let her ass turn into a deformed pumpkin; now the girl has to squeeze into tops that'll make her tits defy gravity. Donna's a perfect companion for clubbing or daytime drinks, such as this. When someone — *anyone* — walks by us, I get off on knowing exactly who they're looking at. Let's be honest, the girl reads *books*, okay? We could never be true BFFs.

The waiter seems startled by my kissy face as I nudge his elbow with my right breast, sliding into the booth. Donna blows me an air smooch. Her face looks like a corn puff: She's been drinking for days.

I fucking love this bitch!

☉

Donna chugs a craft brew as I flick my tongue on a daiquiri straw. She ordered some fried mac-n-cheese bites "for us." She's halfway through her latest date horror when I catch a familiar face down below. Willy is pushing his twisted wife past the churro stand. The woman looks different from this angle, like a squirmy larva stuck in a peach. I feel for him. Least, I try to. Could've sworn the woman was Asian, but from here she is obviously white. Something about being a voyeur always makes me giddy. Willy looks awkward as hell in his dumb cowboy gear. *What the hell is he doing with that poor crip in public?* I've heard him sing a thousand tunes and not one was about this burden.

Donna clears her throat as the appetizer arrives.

"Sorry, babe. What were you saying?"

Donna wolfs a cheese bite and starts back in. I tune her out, deciding that drinks with her today were a bad idea. She'll die alone but refuses to accept it. Why should I have to listen to her pathetic whine? I pretend that my phone buzzed and peer into my purse.

"Oh, shit!"

"What is it?"

"Nothin'. Forgot about something I need to do. *Fuck.*" I tap my acrylics on the cocktail glass before sucking its dregs. "Sorry. I gotta go, hun. Drinks on me next time, 'kay? I'll text." Before Donna can speak through another mouthful, I shoot out the booth with an eyes-closed kissy face and rush for the stairs.

❧

I keep my distance nearing the break wall. A double scoop of fat-free rainbow sherbet helps to conceal my face, doubling as lunch. Willy and his wife are at a far bench, taking in the grandeur of sailboats cutting the bay. I should rephrase that: Willy is seated at the bench while his wife remains in her wheelchair, doing her impression of a dolphin caught in a tuna net.

Don't say it.

I already know.

I'm *sooo* bad.

A drip of ice cream falls between my tits and sends a jolt. I almost yelp but don't want to blow my cover. I spin in a circle, tossing the cone to some gulls in the harbor. That's when I can hear her sobbing. Was this just her daily cry — the wail of the wretched? I could do a dozen pouty frowns right now, but I won't. Salt breeze has me imagining the taste of her tears. *Willy, you poor old fool.*

Maybe it's all the pills, but I kind of feel detached, you know? Last time I cried was when Bowie died — but even then I merely capitalized on an opportunity. Seeing their display makes me sick. Still can't imagine letting someone into my heart *that* close.

Fool me once, cruel world —

❧

There's a little pep in my step tonight, shuttling baby back ribs and Coke refills to hearty eaters, face down in their plates. They snort like hounds given people-food. The only thing that would make this job worse would be if humans devoured their dinners like flies; a cacophony of slurps and regurgitation instead of the usual mindless banter or family feud. Willy is perched on his stool before a mic, grinding away at guitar; his boot taps to the beat of an old Hank tune. Some days he sounds pretty good; I pause in the kitchen to take in the song, reliving that pier-side visual of him and his wife. A creeping headache at the base of my skull lets me know a migraine is coming on. I rub my neck but hear Sal approaching with the new girl and act like I'm busy loading napkins. Saloon doors swing, letting in a sea of giggles. I turn towards them, a sour look on my face to show something's wrong. Sal lets me take an early break. I'm positive he's about to fuck this little slut in his office.

Believe me.

I would know.

☙

The smoker's patio is empty. I contemplate rushing to the Cabriolet to snort a rail but then remember I'm fresh out of Vics. The migraine could be the beginnings of withdrawal, but I pretend it's from stress. The menthol barely hits my lips before the door swings open and out walks Willy with his Zippo. I don't have to ask: his flame is always mine. We smoke in silence for three puffs. His face is much more weathered under the moon's spell. I'm sure I'd cry too if I could see myself in this light.

"I liked that song."

"Which, dear?"

"Dunno what it's called." I hum a few bars and say the only lyrics I recall.

Willy smiles, wrinkles on his face climbing like torn leather. "'Lovesick Blues.' Yeah, that one'll haunt."

Mid-drag, a needle jolts my brain. I wince, and he notices.

"Everythin' alright?"

"Migraine." I drop the smoke to rub my temples.

Willy looks over his shoulder before pulling out a small tin case from his pocket. He opens it, presenting it to me like some engagement ring. "One a these ought to kill it."

With a simple glance, I know exactly what pills they are: little devils that got me into my first stint of rehab. Tommy introduced them to me when I flew out to see him gig Brooklyn. They're pretty hard to come by nowadays. Heroin is much cheaper and that's what sent me spiraling the last time. "Where'd you get these?"

"My wife needs 'em. She suffers from chronic pain — after the accident."

I want to ask about this *accident*, but then I'd have to swallow the pool of saliva I've already gathered to munch this beast. The moment its bitterness caresses my tongue it's like an old friend back to visit.

There's no going back now.

I'm done for.

"Thanks."

He returns the case to his back pocket. "Don't mention it, girl. Always got plenty 'round the house for my sweet Missy."

"Missy? That your wife's name?"

"Yeah."

"That's my daughter's name."

He exhales a plume. "I didn't know you had a child."

"Yeah, well …" I move for the door and tickle his shoulder with my nails. "Thanks again, Willy."

❧

The world is rosy once again. I scratch my nose, taking in the barroom panorama of gnashing teeth and gnarled faces. Sal's not going to like me asking to go home early, but I don't care. An idea has popped into my brain that is clawing like a cornered lobster. I crash open the saloon doors, through the kitchen, and punch into the main office. The new girl is half-clothed and seated on Sal's desk chair. She's been crying (a lot); Sal looks like he's trying to sell her a used car. I tell him my plight, and he doesn't even wince. Protecting his ass in this situation is far more important than little ole me. I toss my apron at one of the fry cooks and hit the bricks.

❧

Donna's down as fuck, so I give her a call. She agrees to meet me at my parents' house: I told her I felt horrible about leaving her today and want to make it up to her. She has no idea what I've got in store.

I pull the Cabriolet into the driveway and hope that none of the house's upstairs lights click on. Luckily, I keep my illusion kit in the glovebox. Don't ask why … I mean, you can imagine. Looks like my old rig case back when I was really hooked; the insides can pick any basic door lock. Hopefully, I won't need to use it. I mean, a knock with this face behind the door is usually good enough. At least, it used to get me backstage when Tommy stopped putting me on the VIP list.

Donna pulls up in her lifted Ford pickup. I eye the house one more time before darting into the street and climbing into the cab. I have a strange feeling that Missy saw me; her curtain shimmered. I block it out. Donna hightails it; I don't even have to ask.

⟐

Willy plays another set in six minutes, so I'll have all the time I need. I navigate Donna through a zigzag of charmless homes off Anza and Sepulveda. That time I saw Willy in the Vons parking lot, I guess I forgot to mention that I followed him in the Cabriolet for most of the day. I like to watch, remember? His house is a modest one-story slathered in bright lavender paint. Home Depot must've had it on clearance or something. Donna parks across the street as I eye the darkened curtains for any sign of life.

"What's going on, Randi?"

"Lemme see your purse."

I remember that she carries this pink stun gun wherever she goes. I swipe it and open the door. The scent of wet grass floats into the cab. I realize this girl deserves some sort of explanation — at least a reason not to ditch me. "I gotta collect some money this bitch owes me. Once I get it, we can go party, 'kay? Don't worry. Everything'll be fine."

"I really gotta pee."

My eyes remain still, but I feel them rolling back into my skull. I can tell by her glassy eyes that a party is already coursing through her veins. She must've kept throwing 'em back at Barney's all day. "Pinch it a little longer, girl. I'll be right quick." I march over Willy's front lawn, destroying a row of petunias. To think Donna drove her truck to pick *me* up in her current state drives me nuts. *What a selfish whore*. I decide not to knock; if the wretch is inside, I'm pretty sure she can't open a goddamn door. I unzip the illusion kit.

Alakazam!

❋

Inside the house it's completely dark, curtains drawn, not even a sliver of moonlight. Smells like my grandpa's last hospital room — the time when Mom made me sit with him while she ran out for a doctor. Can still see that dry tongue spilling out his face. *Just another of life's bad tattoos.* In a far bedroom, I can hear a TV blaring: some talent show with a famous Stones tune being molested. I smack my shin on a poorly placed coffee table and bite down on my lip to prevent an expletive. *Never been in a living room without couches before; prolly from the wheelchair.* Blue light begins to flicker down the hallway. Stun gun in hand, I unlock its safety and wait for a courage that never comes. Thirty seconds feels like hours. I still don't hear a peep — too shaky to check. The wretch is either asleep or captivated by some poor singer about to have his world shattered. I slide the gun into a back pocket and head for the bathroom.

The cabinet above the sink is filled with medical supplies and a tube of Analpram. I wince and head for the kitchen. Mom used to hide her Percocet from me atop our refrigerator. I figure it's a safe bet to search before storming into that bedroom as if it were Black Friday. I tiptoe across linoleum and spot an entire Rubbermaid box filled with beautiful amber vials beside the microwave. Goose flesh tingles up the arms, surging onward to my ears. My itchy nose smells victory.

I attack, careful not to rattle each treasure. This twisted bitch has got it all. I could die happy swallowing one pastel tablet after another; pretty little coffins meant to solve everything — all for *me*! I'm about to glom the whole case when I hear the front door creak open.

I freeze.

A whisper cracks the world.

"Baby girl … I gotta pee."

Fucking Donna! I rush to shush her. That's when I hear it: the end of that horrid song out the TV. Donna is holding her crotch like a toddler; *bitch is good for nothing.* I put a finger to my lips and wave her back outside. She defies me, rushing into the hallway, searching for a bathroom. Her boots click atop wood flooring. I rush after her. Soon as I lunge into the hallway, the far bedroom door opens, illuminating the walls. A Latina in scrubs emerges; in her hands, a bag of BBQ Lays. The sight of me forces a scream from deep inside her.

Why didn't I check the fucking room?

Of course this crip has a nurse when left alone!

I reach for the great equalizer in my back pocket. The girl shoots into the bedroom, slamming the door, locking it shut.

I turn to the kitchen.

The plan is now to grab that case and leave Donna to her own devices. Her piss stream from out the bathroom is like a lion's roar in my ears. I take one lunge backwards and slam into the hallway doorframe. My back pocket ignites, turning the world into a brilliant supernova. I am paralyzed, timbering to the floor. I can see but can't focus — does that make any sense? Something shoots up at me — cracks my neck before I can even pound the ground. *Goddamn coffee table!*

Relief washes greater than high tide.

All pain is killed, consciousness lost.

I am a moon rock.

I feel nothing.

For a life billed as lowbrow gossip, I can only imagine what Mouth Bay thinks of me now. Sure as hell isn't Rock Star. The coma was induced, but I'm pretty sure I would've pulled through. I mean, I always have before. Take it from me: Hack doctors always jack up their hospital tabs. *Whatever*. I'm covered for now thanks to Texas Loosey's; Dad'll put up the house if he has to — at least that's what Mom said. Missy brings me flowers most days but still can't even pull it together to look me in the eyes. I don't blame her. I have yet to gaze into a mirror.

Well, it's not that easy: I can't without being propped.

"From the neck down" is all I remember them saying once I woke up. Can still see that supernova whenever I close my eyes; then again, this cocktail they have me on is the best I've ever tasted. Almost feel my extremities. I smirk thinking that Missy'll call *me* The Wretch from here on out, our caretaking roles now reversed. Oh, shit. I just remembered that Willy's wife's named Missy too. She won't call me a damn thing, since she can't speak. Sometimes life's a pisser. I'll talk again, they think. Willy decided not to file charges after hearing of my perpetual state. What a softy. Donna on the other hand — nevermind... Who fucking cares about that whore? *I'm done for — and so is she — so are all of us!*

The cute RN delivers some apple juice and presses the straw to my dry tongue. His forearms are all veiny like the guys in Mom's trashy novels. I'm sure he had his way with me when I was out cold — I mean, why wouldn't he? I'd let him do it again too. Spread these gams right now if I could, see if I can feel his pressure. *A new illusion to master.* On a more uplifting note, I've lost eighteen pounds!

The RN's attention begins to drift to another patient's call.

Here comes the best part of my day.

I think about never roller skating again and squeeze out a tear. It bombs onto the blue gown tenting my bust. The RN jumps into action, swiping its trail from off my cheek.

To feel his coarse finger almost makes this all worth it.

It's all so simple now, letting go.

One daily cry, and I win.

FOR HIRE

A.S. Youngless

I watched the glittering cars drive down Vermont Avenue from the observation deck on top of the Griffith Observatory. It was a sequence-filled lava flow made of overpriced leases and beaters thirty years past their prime. My chin rested on my forearm, body leaning into the wall designed to stop people from jumping. The wall wouldn't stop me if I wanted to do it. Right then I was okay.

An ambulance worked its way through the traffic. It was a slow push. People were either too busy, too trapped, or too apathetic to move out of its way.

"This her?" the client asked. I didn't recognize his voice. Didn't turn to look him over.

The boxy red and white bus swerved into oncoming traffic. Disco lights on top, telling everyone to get the hell out of the way. I wished I had disco lights. Party all the time. I hadn't celebrated a damn thing in four years. No disco lights for me.

"Yeah, like I explained in my email," Peter said. "She's the muscle. It's simple. You sign the contract, give us half up front. We use it to do a little recon on the target. Night of the full moon, she slips into their home before the change. Night comes and your troubles are dealt with." Peter's voice I knew. He was my "handler." Whatever the hell that meant. Basically, he was the guy my mom left me with when she couldn't stand looking at me anymore. I missed her anyway.

"What is she, like, fifteen?" the guy said.

"Eighteen." Peter paused. The ambulance shimmied back into the correct traffic flow and cut left. My guess was that it turned onto Fountain. It was where they kept all the dying kids boxed up in concrete and glass. It's also where Peter and I first met.

"She's legal," the guy said. "Well, that changes things."

"Don't get any ideas." Peter's voice cut with a hard warning.

I peeked back. Peter, who was barely three inches taller than my five-foot-two body, stood between me and the man. He was trying to keep me safe, even though the client towered over us. I locked eyes with the guy. He was middle-aged but took care of himself. Broad in all the right places, tight in the rest. I guessed he worked out daily. His gaze was heated. I'd seen the look a few times before. It said, *Is it bestiality if she's a werewolf?* My lips pursed, eyes narrowed. His gaze melted into a glare as he tried to look menacing. I knew he wasn't, or he wouldn't have been there in the first place.

I faced them, elbows resting on the ledge while the sound of traffic drifted up the Griffith Park hills, singing its sweet, sweet song. I'd always heard the bent notes in the car horns way before I became a freak of nature.

"Why?" I said, hoping he'd say it out loud. He didn't. He didn't even say, "Why what?" Letting me shoot back, "Why you acting all big and mighty, but you need to hire a kid to do your dirty work?"

I got nothing.

Peter remained a sentry between the man and me. He never gave me the sex stare. It was one of the many reasons I knew he wasn't so bad. In the four years I'd lived with him, he never once tried to touch me. He'd stood up to giants to protect me. Hell, he even took me to In & Out

Burger and let me order off the secret menu even though he hated fast food and didn't eat meat. I liked meat. Still do. Raw, cooked, pureed in a smoothie, it doesn't matter. It's all delicious.

The client wore Ray-Bans and a leather jacket so soft it rolled over his muscles. Judging by the smell, the jacket was made of antelope, one that once preferred the desert over the grasslands. Probably why it ended up a jacket. His shoes probably cost over a grand but were made of goat, and not the special kind that showed up in yoga class. This one was most likely crazy. You know the type. The ones you see videos about, ramming their heads into shit for no reason. That's what his shoes were made from. Crazy goat.

The rest of his outfit was overpriced and plant-based. I didn't care about plants. They all smelled like dirt and the sweat of the people who made them.

"It talks," he snarled, trying to hide his interest. The guy was a sugar-coated candy. Hard and showy on the outside. Gooey and scared in the middle. He could have shown up in a full leather jumpsuit tanned in the markets of Morocco and the scent of his fear and excitement still would have overpowered all the death and manure on the clothes. "Your message said I'd only deal with you." He zoned in on Peter. "And here she is. Why bring her if I'm not allowed to sample the goods?"

I'd pegged him as a producer. A filthy rich one who made mainstream blow-up movies, yet claimed they were art. Not that it mattered how he financed his expensive life. All I cared was that Peter and I got our going rate.

"You *are* dealing with me directly," Peter said, throwing me a look. It said, *shut up*. I shrugged and turned back to watch Vermont's afternoon road show.

When I was little, before the accident, things were different. There was no Peter. Just me and Mom. We didn't live in a second-story walk-up in K-Town but a townhouse in Culver City. There was a pool and a hot tub, and on hot, hot nights she'd take me down when everyone else was asleep and we'd swim until our skin was cool and wrinkly.

"You're my special girl," she'd say and cuddle me close. Her legs whipped back and forth to keep us in the cooling night air. "You're the reason I was born. I know it in my bones." She'd set me on the dry walkway before lifting herself out of the pool. Together we'd slip into the hot tub where I'd fall asleep, forcing her to carry me upstairs, dripping wet.

She said stuff to me like that all the time. "You're the best girl alive, Jenny. You're the smartest girl around. I'm lucky to be your mom. It's why I was born."

I never cared I didn't have a dad or family or friends. I had her. I had my mom. She was a goddess. Until she left.

"Look. I read everything you sent me. Even did some of my own research. I respect your process but would be lying if I said I wasn't surprised by the age and size of your wolf," the client said. I guessed his assistant did the research or maybe he asked his virtual assistant. The virtual one probably liked him better, mostly because she didn't have any emotions.

Peter bristled. He pulled himself up and shoved a finger into the giant's chest. "Size isn't an issue. She does good work."

"According to you."

"Listen. Either you want to hire her or not. It's that simple. Yes or no." His head shook before grabbing my arm and tugging me off the wall. "Nevermind. This was a mistake. I broke a rule agreeing to meet you. No Hollywood types. You're all overprivileged pains in the asses." He tugged me along, not that I put up much of a fight. Mostly he caught me by surprise.

When we reached the stairs, he let go. I turned to see how the client was handling our overly dramatic exit. His sunglasses hid any chance of catching a real reaction. I flipped him off and started down the steps.

Hands in pockets, I followed Peter down the hill in search of our car. I'd always wanted to drive up the road James Dean and Natalie Wood rolled up on in *Rebel Without a Cause*, but it was one way. The wrong way. Peter said drawing any unwanted attention was bad.

"Why'd we come if you weren't going to let me do the job?" I asked in a sulky voice. The wind kicked up, a plastic bag wrapped around my ankle, grit from the canyon speckled my face. "Usually I don't meet the clients until after the full moon. Not before."

"He's a pervert. You're not working for a pervert." He held his key fob out, pressing the unlock button. Nothing beeped. "I didn't realize we parked so far down the hill."

A black minivan with a glittery "Soccer Mom" sticker slowed near us. The passenger window rolled down.

"Are you leaving?" a pretty blonde lady asked. Her nervousness flitted out of the car, carrying on the canyon breeze to me. Some people took parking way too seriously.

"Can't find the car," I shouted. She rolled the window up and drove off. "Anyone who contacts you for my services is never on the up-and-up. So, he's a pervert. Not like he was the first one to give me that look, and it's not like he could do anything about it. Plus, it's fifty g's, and since you won't let me hit up Broadway Federal, we gonna need to get some bling some other way."

Peter stopped abruptly, and I tripped into him. "They're not all the same."

"Molly wanted me to eat her husband." I arched a brow, foot kicking at a flattened to-go cup. There was a trash can ten steps away; it irked me how lazy people were.

I snatched up the cup and dropped it in the can, staring him down as I waited for his explanation.

Peter threw up his hands. "Who beat her for the last ten years." He shifted closer as a conga line of tourists pushed past us snapping photos of the Hollywood sign and the observatory.

"Fine." I slammed my fists into my hips, elbow barely missing them. They inched closer to the chain-link fence with an eye roll in our direction. "What about Damari?"

"What about him?" Peter reached out his arm, key fob pointing into the distance. He pressed the button and we were greeted by a beep and the flash of taillights. "Finally."

"He had three hits on his list. Three." I held up three fingers.

Peter turned to me again. I waited.

"Ped-o-philes." He broke the word into syllables. "Kind of like Mr. Hollywood up there." He started walking, leaving me to follow in his wake. "He was a mistake. Won't happen again. We only let people hire us who really need our help."

"You mean poor people."

"They're not all poor. Regardless, doesn't it feel nice to help those who need it?" he said over his shoulder. I stared at his blue and gray flannel hugging his puffy body. Peter never understood wife beaters and pedophiles still tasted like shit. All humans tasted like shit. Yet there I was. *Helping*. I lifted my gaze to the heavens. The full moon waited in the afternoon sky.

"Is that the same minivan?" Peter said. I glanced down the road, certain it couldn't be. How could she get all the way down and back again before we found the Prius? But it was. The sun hit the "Soccer Mom" sticker just right. The window began to descend, and I smelled it — desert antelope and crazy goat. A hand extended out the side of the van, fingers wrapped around a gun.

"Peter!" I screamed too late. Two lights flashed from the minivan window as the gun fired. Copper and iron overpowered the animal scents. Peter fell backward, landing at my feet. My hands pressed against my heart as I watched two black holes bubble over, red with blood.

"Jenny," he bit out. "Run." Red bloomed over the blue and gray plaid.

The minivan's sliding door opened. A bag covered my head. Something hit my temple. Darkness.

☾

I woke inside a dog kennel. My arms and legs were tied in a way that curled me into an unnatural backbend. Rope cut into my skin. From the smell of it, someone pulled out a mastiff seconds before they shoved me in the cage.

I looked around as well as I could. The cage was in a mud room — you know, one of those extra rooms adults like to pretend keep the rest of the house clean. Every inch of the place smelled of dirty shoes, unwashed dog, urine, and humans.

"What if she doesn't change?" a woman said from the other room.

"He said she'll transform at dusk. Is it dusk yet?" Mr. Hollywood shouted. My mind went to Peter, on the side of the road, bleeding. He had been alive when I left him. I prayed he was in a hospital. I needed to get to him to make sure he was all right.

"Obviously not, Craig. Still, you should have thought this through. There are other ways to get rid of Liza. Less complicated ones," the woman replied. The one from the van. Pretty and photo-ready.

I glanced out the window. There were roughly three hours until sunset when I transformed.

"Oh, look. The bitch is awake." He appeared with his smug expression and languid words. "A female dog is a female dog, am I right?" His pristine white button-down was unbuttoned one too many holes, displaying graying chest hair and a gold chain. His leather jacket was missing, but his sunglasses were still in place. Asshole. "Does the puppy want a bone?" A generic milk bone dropped past my nose. I cringed and turned away.

"Where's Peter?" I hissed through clenched teeth. "If you killed him — "

"Don't worry, little girl. He's still alive, for now." Craig stared down at me. "But for kicks, what would you do?" I couldn't do anything until sunset. He outweighed me by some hundred-fifty pounds, easily. Reading my thoughts, he lowered, reached through the kennel, and grabbed my chin. I stared at my reflection in his smoky gray lenses. He was close enough for me to see his eyes, crinkled in the corners, pupils wide and excited, matching his scent.

"You won't be here when it's time. I have a special lady for you to meet." His hand glided down my face and onto my shoulder. Fingers probing the fleshy parts of my over-extended joint. His lips parted, a breath escaped.

"I have to know," he said, nearly panting. "Do you like it doggy style?" His hand slid towards my breast. I buckled, throwing my full weight back, and wrapped my mouth around his hand. Teeth bared, I clamped on hard. Blood spilled into my mouth. He tasted horrible, but I lapped up his blood with a smile, just to piss him off.

"Fucking cunt." He reeled, hand catching on the bars. When he was free he kicked the cage, screaming until the woman came in. "She bit me," he snarled. "The bitch bit me."

My tongue flickered out of my mouth, licking his blood off my lips. It was deep, he'd need stitches. Good.

"Come on, Craig. I have some ointment in the bathroom."

They moved into the main part of the house, leaving me caged and tied in the mudroom.

"If Peter's dead, I'll do more than bite you next time," I shouted.

My body went as slack as the ropes allowed. I hated the full moon. Each month was the same. A new job and me remembering my mom. It was my fault: I was a monster and she left. I sighed as the mastiff sauntered into the room. He sat next to the cage, staring for a second before he leaned forward licking my face.

"Good boy," I purred. "You need a better owner, don't you, big guy?" He licked me a second time, reminding me of when I wanted to be a veterinarian. The kind who worked with big animals. Fourteen-year-old me figured no one cared enough about them.

"You think you can open the cage?" I said to the dog. He stared with his big wrinkled face and droopy eyes, letting me know he wouldn't ever be in the cage if he could. "Yeah, stupid question." I stared at him, not wanting to think about Peter dying or my mom, but he looked like a dog at the rescue farm in Santa Clarita she took me to. The place had been jam-packed with one of every farm animal I could imagine. It was a dream come true. I told Mom to forget my birthday and Christmas. That single day was every gift I wanted, every dream fulfilled. I was certain I'd be a vet, and I hugged a cow for good luck. Then I ate lunch with a pig, fed some ducks and chickens, and even played fetch with a three-legged mastiff named Buddy.

I looked the dog over. This one had all four legs. I doubted Craig and the blonde lady rescued a dog in their lives. They gave off more of a puppy-mill kind of vibe. The dog huffed before it lay down by the cage. Down the hall, Craig cried. The woman mumbled something about disinfectant. I hoped the wound would go septic.

"Seriously," I said to the dog. "After this, you should come live with me." The dog quirked a brow and huffed again.

I could take him to a farm, I thought, and then shook my head. The last time I'd been near a farm I'd been so happy I refused to leave until the staff made me. Then, in the parking lot, I begged my mom to wait even longer.

She allowed it. She in her shin-length summer dress, brown hair pulled back. The sun set behind her and she glowed, all angelic.

It was the last perfect moment in my life.

She loved me so much, and I made her hate me. If I'd just gotten into the damn car and gone home when she wanted to, but no. The visit wasn't enough, I had to stay longer. That greed was the very reason I was tied up in a dog crate. If I'd just listened, if I'd just gotten into the car when she told me to, maybe then she wouldn't have been so angry with me. Maybe then she wouldn't have sent Peter to deliver the message she didn't want me anymore. Could-a, should-a, would-a …

"Hey. Maybe go get help? What do you think about that, big guy?" The dog didn't flinch. He slept as if I wasn't in his space.

Craig stormed into the room. The mastiff jumped up and ran out the doggie door.

"It's time to do your job," he said, kicking the bars. The cage slid back a few inches, rolling me in the dog urine coating the floor. "I don't give a rat's ass what you do when you're done. Run off into the park or jump off the goddamn observatory. I don't give a shit. Just do the job and understand that if I see you ever again, I'll kill you. Got it?"

Craig's arm was wrapped in a bandage, bits of brownish red dotting the tan fibers.

I smiled, a small smile that barely reached my eyes.

"I said, do you understand?" He spat the words at me as he dug his fingers into his pants pocket. "Do you see this?" He held up a single silver bullet.

"Yes."

"Then say you understand."

"Oh, I get it."

"Good." He tucked the bullet away.

"Here's hoping I don't see you first." I winked. Craig glanced around, grabbed a bucket of brackish water, and dumped it on me. Then he dragged the cage, and me along with it, outside to load into the minivan.

I couldn't see where we were headed, only felt every bump in the road. Each one slammed me against the cage and the cage against the side of the van. Craig turned up music, drowning out my grunts. I counted seven songs before we stopped. He pulled me from the cage and tossed me to the ground. The aroma of eucalyptus and citrus blossoms hit me, dulling the mastiff's odor. The new scents meant we'd left the coastal plain and were in the Valley. I looked around, trying to pinpoint my location. There they were, the Santa Monica Mountains looming in the west. Long fingers of tangerine and purple poked out above their peaks, painting the few clouds that made it through the day. In front of me was a mini-mansion. It stood out against the old Spanish-style homes waiting to be knocked down for progress.

"That one." He pointed at the dark gray exterior. My gaze drifted to the red door. I didn't know who the target was, why I was there, or what he or she had done to deserve death by werewolf. Peter normally handled that part. Peter. If he died, I'd rip Craig to shreds, silver bullet or not. I wanted to tear out Craig's throat. The lower the sun dropped, the more I wanted to lick his bones clean.

My skin prickled. It was starting.

"What if I don't want to?" I didn't.

Craig lifted his gun, high enough for me to see, but tucked near his hip so onlookers didn't spot it right away. Sulfur, saltpeter, with a hint of urine — the big three notes of a recently fired gun — wafted in my direction. It was the gun he used to shoot Peter. He unloaded the clip, pulled the silver bullet from his pocket, added it to the waiting bullets, and pushed the clip back inside.

"He's not dead," Craig said as he leveled the gun on me. "The little fat man who parades you around is in intensive care over at Cedars. If you don't go in there and do what I say, I'll shoot you first and then I'll go finish him off."

Even confidence has a scent. His was overpowering. If he could smell my confidence, it would have crushed his. My nostrils flared, lip curling, showing him my human teeth that weren't so human anymore.

I imagined Peter in the long thin bed, blanket tucked around his round body, tubes in his face and hands. It's how I looked when he found me after I'd been attacked at the farm. He'd been my orderly extraordinaire. Even sat with me every night. My savior who took me in after my mom left. I asked him about her. Asked him every single day for a month. He always said the same, "She left you. You remember that. Always. It'll keep you alive and strong." Peter would finish his speech the same way. "Remember she didn't want you because you were mangled. Do you honestly think she'd take you back now that you're a dog?"

The answer was no.

Craig cocked the gun to drive his point home. "I'm not bluffing."

I didn't believe Peter when he told me she abandoned me. I couldn't, but then he showed me how she moved from Culver to Venice by the canals. Each time I questioned him about her, he showed more proof. The last time he handed me his phone, I saw an image of her and a baby on the screen. This time she'd had a son. I hid under the covers of my bed for two days after that bomb.

Peter became my rock, the person to get my back, and now this guy with his overpriced life wanted to take him from me.

I glanced down the street and held up my hands. "I believe you. Just leave Peter alone, okay?"

I rarely went to the Valley. It was too hot, and that day was no exception. I lowered my hands, standing tall, best as I could. My spine curved between my shoulder blades. Dog spine. It was nearly dark and the moon was inching its way higher.

"Tell me." I nodded towards the house.

"Liza," he said, shoving a blouse under my nose. I turned away after catching the scent of roses and saline. "Mid-thirties." He handed me a photo. A pretty Latina woman with a wide grin. A tuft of black hair rested against her chest. I didn't know who the hair belonged to, the photo had been cut in half. "Her and anyone with her."

"Why? What she do?" I asked, vainly.

His lips pressed into a white line. He wasn't talking.

I couldn't do it, couldn't kill that woman. Craig didn't need to know, not until I figured out my next move. My hand dropped as I looked up the block. I didn't know the house or the neighborhood. I had no real way out and now he wanted me to kill multiple victims without any explanation.

"This won't work," I said. "I'm already changing. I should be inside."

He was less careful with the gun, holding it high and near my face.

"The silver bullet for you and the rest of the clip for Peter."

The sun was gone, the moon a white disk in the sky. My electric skin buzzed as my bones grew, twisted, turning me into the thing he really hired in the first place. Craig watched, inching back the more my new form appeared. My nails turned to claws, nose into a snout. Skin exploding with tufts of hair. My clothes ripped, releasing the wolf they trapped.

His eyes widened, gun shaking, its barrel aimed at me. "Liza," he shouted, motioning to the house as he scurried to his car. "Go get her." The mini-van glowed in the moonlight. The door swung open and he slipped inside.

I sniffed the air. Craig's scent clung inside my nostrils, blocking out the eucalyptus and citrus. Liza's wasn't far off as I started for the house. I didn't move quickly, not then. There was a time for fast. Stalking was never it.

A nightingale chirped then fell silent as I approached the tree it was perched in. My stomach twisted. A nightingale was less than an appetizer.

Head tilted to one side, I watched the house. A breeze kicked up, running over my fur. Peter didn't know I liked me after I changed. I liked the fur and the teeth. It was armor. He also didn't know I was lucid until the hunger hit. I let him believe the movies — I was a monster from the second I changed. Some secrets were okay.

I sensed movement inside the house. Liza shuffling around. She didn't know I was there — watching. No one did. The street was a graveyard, empty as a void. My nails clicked on the asphalt and then on the cement driveway. Grass scratched the pads of my feet, dry and dying. I was surprised there was any, but we were in the Valley. People watered in the Valley.

The closer I stalked, the more pungent her scent. I circled the house; it was strongest near the side — next to her car. A dark gray mid-sized family sedan, car seat included.

My stomach burned. Hungry. I smelled a dog, two streets over, one of those toy breeds. I could go there and eat it, but Craig was waiting with a bullet for me, the rest for Peter. I threw my weight at the door, again and again. The wood splintered, hinges bending. Beyond it, fear laced the air, mingled with the scent of Liza. She screamed, paralyzed, watching me. The blood-curdling kind. They all screamed the same way. I was a monster, one that should only exist on television or in films. Yet, there I was, on her doorstep.

Broken wood in shards and slivers covered the floor both inside and out, glass glistening in the night air. I rushed inside. Agile, sure-footed, I chased her through the house, finding her before she could hide behind a paltry, hollow thing she used as a bedroom door. Teeth bare, spittle dripped in thick drops. My haunches high, fur on end.

She looked nice. Pretty with thick black hair like a silky oil slick hanging over her shoulders.

"No," she pleaded, hands out in front of her. "Help," she screamed. "Somebody, help me!"

I snapped. My heart slammed into my ribs, snarling and growling. The longer I hesitated, the more human and normal she was. I came up to her waist; if I wanted to do the job, it would have been easy. All the others threw things at me. All the others had weapons out as if they knew I was coming.

No one ever knew I was coming.

A cry came from the back of the room. Small. New.

I stopped and waited. This was who Craig wanted me to kill? A woman and a baby?

I started forward. Slow. Deliberate. Soft wails punctured the air. I spotted the bassinet. One single hand reached out, a tiny fist pumping into the sky.

"You leave him alone," Liza shouted. "Stay away from him."

She rushed at me. A lamp in hand to use as a weapon.

I twisted back, snapping at her. She backed down, only for a second, only until I turned for the bassinet again. Then she ran at me. I snapped at her again, until she understood I'd rip her hand off. Inside the cradle, two round black eyes stared up at me. A tuft of blackish hair, like in the photo Craig showed me. The baby wore a Rams jersey and a diaper, little toes uncovered, hands wrapped in socks.

I couldn't do it. A silver bullet wasn't enough to get me to eat a baby. Peter would have to understand. My stomach churned, the hunger tearing its way through my body. I had to leave. To get out. If I stayed much longer, the hunger would become blinding and I'd eat anyone. Even a baby.

I leaned in, long pink tongue sliding along the baby's face. He giggled. Liza didn't. She threw the lamp, hitting me in my shoulder blades. It was a good hit. I fell, quickly stood up and reminded myself there was a chow-chow two streets over. A dog was better than a baby. I needed to leave before I messed up, before I did something I couldn't undo.

Liza edged towards me, hand extended, testing me. My stomach hurt, bad. It knotted, too tight to breathe through. I stumbled into the hall, legs kicking the floor. If I didn't kill Liza, Craig would end Peter and me. I couldn't kill her or the kid. Wouldn't.

My legs wobbled as the hunger deepened. I tripped into a wall, shook my head for clarity, and sprinted to the door. The scent of antelope and goat hit me like a wall. Craig, in the driveway, cell phone in one hand, the gun with its silver bullet in the other.

I stopped, dropping low in front, ready to charge. Liza paused behind me, baby in her arms; her fear was palpable. It wasn't all for me, part of it spiked at the sight of Craig. I stepped between her and him, his gun aimed at my skull. She stepped back, twisting to shield the baby with her body.

"Craig?" Liza stuttered. "Craig! The dog's trying to kill Jose." Craig swung the gun around, aiming it at her. Then it hit me like a wall. Shit, it was his baby. Stupid Liza. "What are you doing?"

"Why aren't you doing your job?" he hollered at me.

My stomach clenched. I was out of time.

"Don't do this, Craig." Her voice wavered. "Leave me and Jose alone," she begged. "We won't bother you. It'll be like we're not even here."

Peter had been right. Craig was a waste of a job. We didn't help people like him, we helped people like Liza.

I edged towards Craig, teeth bared, stomach so empty I picked my dinner then and there. The chow-chow would be happy to know it was off my menu. I snapped at the full entree in front of me. My paws pressed into the concrete and I launched forward. I slammed into Craig's slimy body. As my teeth latched onto his throat, the gun fired, discharging the silver bullet. He missed. I bit down harder and dragged him away from the house, away from Liza and the baby. Then I began to feast, ripping and tearing him apart. The taste of his flesh should have made me gag.

It tasted divine.

He struggled, metal pressing into my fur. Something slammed into his head. I pulled my muzzle back and found Liza with a baseball bat. Jose's cries grew louder; she must have set him down inside. She glanced between me and the door. I barked in the same direction and went back to filling my belly full of Craig.

I mauled his face, teeth dragging over his skull. Then I ate his hands, starting with the one he used to shoot Peter and punched me with. His lips were red, lined with blood, a bubble of air popped into his mouth. He tasted like anger and doubt. I pulled him apart, piece by piece until I heard a scream.

Behind me was a woman and the chow-chow, out for a late-night walk.

I jumped off Craig; his outsides were now a perfect copy of how hollow he was inside. I turned to run. Too many people were watching. Too many questions would be asked.

"Wait!" It was Liza. Little Jose was still crying. He was scared.

Another cry, this one from behind me. Liza yelled stop, but a brick hit me in the head anyway, and the night sky spun, a whirling star cyclone.

☾

Beeping woke me. The shuffling of feet. Metal rings pulled across a metal rod. I flexed my hand and flinched. An IV needle pressed against my vein until I straightened my fingers. Crap. I was in a hospital.

"The mystery girl awakes." An unfamiliar voice. "And how do you feel?" a middle-aged woman with long black hair said. She checked the machines around my bed, typing things into the tablet as she went. I didn't answer. Didn't know how I ended up in a hospital bed wearing a gown.

"Where am I?" I tilted my head to read her name badge. She turned away, moving it from my sightline. When she spun around, cocked a hip, and stared me down, I read the name Kumi Abe.

"I have so many questions for you, but I'll answer yours first. You're in Valley Presbyterian, a woman called 911, got a bus to bring you in two days ago."

I shot up. Hospital sheet fell to my lap. Nurse Kumi set a hand on my shoulder, pushing me back down. "Take it easy. Whomever the good Samaritan was, she called in the nick of time." She paused, searching my face for clues. "She saved you."

If Craig was still alive, I'd eat him again for getting me into this mess.

Nurse Kumi's hand slid off my shoulder, concern deepening the creases around her eyes. "Now I need some answers. Like, what's your name?"

My brow twitched. I didn't want to give her my name, not until I was certain what she knew. Before I did, I wasn't telling her anything. All I knew was I was still in the Valley, which was unfortunate for myriad reasons. The biggest of which was Peter lying in his own hospital bed on Beverly Boulevard, a whole world away. I was on my own. Twice in three days.

"Let's come back to that one. How about, what's the last thing you remember?"

I clutched the sheet with both fists, balling it under my chin. The scent of the sterile hospital mixed with limited options dropped my heart into my stomach. "I don't know," I said, eyes welling up, perfectly.

Nurse Kumi smoothed my hair from my face, questions vanishing. She was a nice lady. I felt bad for playing her. Mostly.

"It's okay, sweetie. We'll help you figure everything out. Just rest." Nurse Kumi stepped out. She paused with the door half-open, speaking to someone out of my sightline.

A shoulder appeared draped in the darkest blue known to humankind. LAPD. My weighted stomach flipped. Kumi's head turned as she spoke with someone else before the door swung back open. "There's someone here to see you."

Panic smoothed into confusion. Why were the police there? I braced myself as Kumi pushed the door open. Instead of the police, I saw a figure, female, brunette, and one-hundred-percent my estranged mother.

The last time I'd seen her was two weeks before Peter told me I was going home with him. He brought me new clothes: jeans two sizes too big and a bright pink over-sized tee that read, "Venice Beach California," with an image of Arnold Schwarzenegger flexing on it.

She left me, a mutant monster, with a total stranger — yet there she was, not ten feet away.

The first time I changed, Peter was ready. We took a bus to the Ranger's Office in Griffith Park and hiked in with a backpack of food. We hid in one of the old zoo exhibits, bending back the fencing and crawling inside where only the homeless would find us. The scent of human urine overwhelmed me.

"It's not so bad, plus, you're safe here." Peter patted the ground.

Right then, in the hospital room, my mom looked nearly the same as I'd last seen her, with bonus strands of silver in her hair and extra crow's feet around her eyes. I'd thought of her so often. Wondered what she was up to. Why she left. I mean, Peter showed me all his proof, but there was always a part of me that refused to believe any of it.

I didn't want to believe it that day at Griffith Park.

"What if I don't change?" I'd asked him. "What if you're wrong about me?"

"You will. Trust me."

Trust me.

I had. I trusted Peter. Yet, after everything he'd told me — there she was, eyes brimming with tears. A mixture of shock and joy holding her face still.

"Jenny?" Mom's voice hadn't changed. It was still honey and sunshine. "Oh my god. It's really you," she stuttered. "After all this time …" she said to Nurse Kumi.

"She hasn't confirmed her —"

"Mom?" I cut off Kumi. Head shaking, eyes blinking, each time they opened she was still there. Words curled around my tongue, choking my throat, and never leaving my lips. They transformed into sobs.

I thought of my first job. It was the second time I transformed. Peter spoke of saving people. He wove stories, sad and heartbreaking. The parents were terrible — like my mom. They hurt their kids — like my mom. No one would listen to them because they were children, not even the police. Real life wasn't like movies. You couldn't have people killed without getting caught. The police always figured it out. Guns were traceable.

"Wolves are not. No one would suspect a person who was mauled had been a murder for hire," he said.

He had a lot of good points. I didn't want people to feel as sad as me. So, I did what he said.

"I've been looking for you for years." Mom moved further into the room but stayed far enough back to give me space. There were dark circles under her eyes. Pools of black, developed over time. "I called the police, they found nothing. I hired a private investigator. He ended up getting mauled by a coyote. Then out of nowhere, the hospital calls me."

"You left me." I gripped the sides of the bed.

Her head shook. "No, I never left you. I would never leave you, Jenny." Tears, crystal and full, spilled down her perfect face.

"But you did. Peter said you couldn't cope. You didn't want me, because …" I pointed at my stomach, at the scar we both knew lay hidden under the hospital gown. "Then you had another baby."

Shock. Pure and simple. "I don't have any other children. There was only you."

"But I saw a photo."

She moved next to the bed, so close I smelled her like a normal girl. One who wasn't a wolf. "If you saw me with a child, it was the neighbors' son. I watch him once in a while if their babysitter is late."

Peter showed me the photo right before he convinced me to go after the pedophiles. He showed more images of the victims. Not of the bad stuff, he told me about those parts pared down. I was already angry with my mom moving on without me, and I agreed on the spot.

"I don't want them hurting more kids."

I felt like a queen after it was done. I'd taken on three guys. Well, two guys and a woman who would never hurt anyone ever again.

My mom would never do something so horrible. But seeing her with a new baby seconds before he brought up the job … It hurt. I wanted to take my hurt and use it on others. So, I did.

My heart broke, a million icy pieces warming as they fell. She didn't have a son. Only me. I moved over, Mom crawled into the bed next to me, arm tucked around my shoulders. We cried. Nurse Kumi pulled the curtains and closed the door, giving us privacy. Most things I said were unintelligible. She smoothed my hair and said, "I know, sweetie. I'm here now." Or "You're safe, sweetie. I love you, so much."

I burrowed against her, cheek below her shoulder. My hand with the IV draped across her. We cried ourselves to sleep. I woke to her heart beating against my cheek. She was there. She didn't leave me.

The monitors flickered. I thought of Peter at Cedars, resting in his own hospital bed. Why had I believed him? My stomach went sour as everything fell into place. Reality was its own full moon; the truth, its own monster. I shifted, holding my mom tight, replaying every moment with Peter. From the hospital to our last job.

"Have you ever met anyone else, you know, like me?" I asked him two months before we met Craig at the observatory. He sat on the plaid sofa, piles of cash stacked on the old coffee table. I was near the window, chin on my knees.

He held up a finger and stopped counting. He was irritated I'd spoken. Peter didn't like to be disturbed when he was working. Most times he ignored me until I went to my room. It was different that day. He paused, glancing up.

"Actually, yes," he said. "A long time ago. A guy I met in Yosemite. We used to do these kinds of jobs, too." His gaze returned to the cash. After he finished counting he'd split it into three piles, one for me, one for him, and a third for a safe deposit box at Broadway Federal Bank on Wilshire. My pile was the smallest. Pocket money so that I could buy things I liked, he said. He covered food, rent, and new clothes to replace the ones I lost during the transformation.

My mom snored, one time. Then she shifted, pulling me closer. I was a traitor for believing Peter. I didn't deserve one second of the hug. I would never give up her hugs, again.

I remembered the day Peter told me about the other wolf because he never mentioned another. Not in the four years we worked together. But it made sense. How else would he know how to set up jobs? It wasn't his first rodeo, and I hadn't been his first wolf.

"What happened to him?" I wanted to know. I felt invincible after I turned. Yes, werewolves had their weaknesses — even Craig knew it — but they were few.

"Sometimes, Jenny ... Why does it matter what happened to him? If you trust me, then you should know you're safe. Right?" He shook his head at me. Disappointment rolling his brow into a series of lines. "All your interruptions keep making me lose count."

"But what happened to him?"

He turned to me, locking eyes. "Look, we did good work, me and him. Just like you and I do. But sometimes jobs go sideways. We had a client who wasn't on the up-and-up." He threw up his hands, growled low in the back of his throat. "Can I finish now?"

Up until Craig, every client we worked with jumped hurdles to get with us. Peter never permitted shortcuts. He created a security checklist, used it for every single job. He didn't use it with Craig.

When my mom woke, I told her everything. From the second I moved in with Peter to waking up in the hospital. She listened to every word. "You won't have to see him, ever again."

But I would and I knew it. The police asked if either of us wanted to press charges against Peter for using my survivor's guilt against me to lure me away from mom, aka kidnapping. We said yes.

I waited for them to bring up Craig, but they didn't. Why would they? It hardly seemed plausible that a teen-aged girl would have anything to do in the mauling death of a local studio executive. According to the news, his death was a tragic coyote attack. Animal Services would diligently track down the animal and destroy it.

"I'll speak with my lawyer and have the police deal with Peter," my mom said the day I was discharged.

"No, Mom. I'll deal with him," I said, dressing in a new set of clothes she'd bought me. "I'm not letting him get away with what he did to us. No way in hell."

Mom said some stuff. The kinds of things you say when you're worried you'll lose the thing you just found again. She wouldn't lose me. There was no way to convince her of it. Worry and fear smelled similar, almost how love and hate have nearly the same notes. Love is sweeter, while hate burns in a cinnamon and cayenne cloud.

"Jenny." Hands on my shoulders, holding me at arm's length. "Please."

I smiled, lips pressed together. "It'll be different. This time I know better."

I had my own security checklist. First, I moved back with my mom. Then, I made some calls to see how Peter was. The hospital told me squat. So, I found a guy who liked my smile. He worked in the kitchen and wanted to impress me. He told me, Peter was recovering. Complications from the gunshot wounds. He'd be home in a few weeks.

In time for the full moon.

Mom drove me to K-Town. She insisted on waiting. I begged her not to. She wouldn't have it. I snuck into his apartment. It wasn't mine, not anymore, even if I knew where the spare key was. The hidden one left for me to use after I changed back into human form. The hospital discharged him earlier in the day. I beat him home by an hour, waited in my room. My *fake* room, I reminded myself.

Keys jingled. He shuffled inside.

"Peter," I said as he walked by my door. He jumped, a hand clutching the wound. I wondered if Craig missed on purpose or by accident. I'd have to live without knowing, seeing he was dead and all.

"Jesus, Jenny," Peter said, letting the sight of me settle around him. "God, I thought Craig killed you."

"Other way around." I motioned as I spoke, reading his body language. He was shocked at the sight of me, surprised I wasn't dead. "He tried to kill me. Had a silver bullet. Told me he'd use it if I didn't kill a woman and a little baby and then he'd finish you off."

"Oh, yeah?" he said, recovering his composure. Small amounts of fear wafted towards me.

"Yeah, but you will be proud of me. They weren't like the others, Peter. They were innocent. So, I attacked Craig." I stood, opening the window in the small bedroom. "Then all this crazy stuff happened and I ended up in a hospital." I paused. "In the Valley." Paused again. "Oh, and Mom showed up."

He waved for me to stop. "Jesus, Jenny. I'm tired and the painkillers are wearing off," he said. Then I smelt it. Full-blown terror. He knew I knew the truth.

He said, "I need to go to bed."

The sun was nearly down. It turned the few clouds to sherbet as the sky darkened.

"Okay, Peter," I said, lips in a huge smile. He started walking. I waited until he was nearly past the door and then said, "But first, can you tell me about Mom, again? Why she left me with you?"

His feet slid to a stop, heart racing. My skin prickled. It was starting. Peter faced me.

"God, Jenny. The bitch didn't want you. End of story."

I made a tsking sound. "I know you're lying. I've *seen* her."

The sun was a tight line on the horizon. Its glow backlit the room. The hair on my neck stood. Peter stared, slowly understanding what was happening.

"Blue moon," I said, voice warbled as the wolf pushed its way to the surface. My head rolled back, the disks between each vertebra popped as my body transformed. "Was Craig part of your plan to get rid of me?" My throat closed, words turned into guttural sounds. The clothing I wore ripped from my body, releasing my wolf.

Peter stumbled, tripping into the wall across the hall. "It wasn't a setup," he sputtered.

I didn't buy it and snapped my reply.

"We had a good thing going, why would I turn on you?"

I charged. He yelped. I pinned him.

"Craig was an idiot, a mistake, Jenny. You need to believe me." Don't. Don't. Don't. Don't. He begged. He cooed at me. He called me a good girl. It really didn't matter if he wanted Craig to kill me; I wouldn't forgive him for tricking me and my mom. He stole four years of my life. Why? Because he liked the money.

When I didn't move, the words changed. He called me a bitch. I was the worst mistake he'd ever made. He said he regretted taking me in. If he could do it over again, he would leave me with my *dumb broad of a mother so she could deal with my bullshit condition.*

"Your kind has one purpose and one purpose only. Face it, I helped you live to your fullest potential," he said. To him, I was a job, and I knew once I was gone, he'd go find another wolf.

I lifted his shirt and dragged my claws down his chest, infecting him. On the next full moon, he would transform, finally becoming the beast he loved to extort so much. Now he could live his own life to its *fullest potential* and I could live mine however I wanted.

It wasn't the plan Mom and I made, but I liked it better than Peter dead. I went to the window and howled. She appeared in the door a few minutes later.

We took what we needed and left.

❧

After Peter, I didn't want to work anymore. Didn't want to taste the shit that was human flesh. I had four years to make up with my mom. We took the money Peter stashed in the apartment and everything in his safety deposit box at Broadway Federal and bought a house on the edge of Griffith Park. With the park butting up against our property it meant I had access to over four thousand acres, right in the middle of the city. I loved it. It wasn't the ranch of my childhood dreams: it was better.

"Jenny," Mother called from the house. "Say goodbye before you go."

The one thing I learned from Peter was I wasn't alone. There were others, like me. Not so much in L.A., but Yosemite wasn't far. Mom said she'd take me there after the winter thaw. Until then, Griffith Park would be my stomping ground, and frozen turkeys and chicken would be my meals.

I didn't know what happened to Peter. Now and then I smelled him nearby, but he never came close. I wondered if he hired himself out? Maybe he did. Maybe he locked himself in the cages at the old L.A. Zoo. I didn't care enough to find out. I'd only care if he crossed into my territory. As long as he didn't, I was happy. I didn't want to mess up my perfect life with my mom. Not again. I turned my back to the park and walked into our kitchen to peck her on the cheek. Whatever he was up to, I hoped he would stay away. My happiest thought was knowing I'd never have to kill anyone ever again.

LETTING GO

Gabi Lorino

Saying goodbye to my only friend at work hit me harder than I thought it would. It seemed strange to even be in that position. Here I was in Southern California, a place known for its friendly inhabitants, and yet somehow I'd ended up in an odd, hostile working environment.

"Good luck at KP," I said. We sat at the outdoor picnic tables near our building and enjoyed a breeze while eating our respective lunches. Karla liked all things Italian — she even drove a Fiat — so I'd brought her a big box of Toblerone as a going-away gift, and she'd allowed herself to have one piece already. "I'm jealous of you, getting to work from home. It's gotta be better than …"

I didn't need to finish my thought. She knew.

"How long do you think you'll last here?" she asked.

I shrugged. "I think you're supposed to stay a year, for the sake of appearance, right?"

"I guess," she said, not sounding convinced. "The proposal cycle just ended. You need another assignment."

"Definitely." I nodded in agreement.

We walked through the campus after we ate. Karla would be barred from entry once she turned her badge in, so it was her last chance to see what we'd helped create. We only had access to some areas, but what we could see was pretty amazing — roped-off experimental vehicles in the reception area; rockets being assembled in brightly lit clean labs; and the giant wall of glowing screens surrounded by rows of desks that looked like something out of a sci-fi movie.

"I remember seeing this place on TV, a while ago," I said as I gazed at what I guessed would be called "mission control."

"It seemed so glamourous, before we worked here," Karla added. "This all looks so cool, yet we work in an ancient office building with asbestos warnings on the door."

"Where everything is somehow the color of dust," I added.

We laughed, then walked in companionable silence back to our office. When I reached to open the office door, Karla tapped my shoulder and asked, "Are you going to be okay? I mean, after this."

I shrugged and looked up at the cloudless blue sky. "I really don't know. I've learned so much that it would be a shame to leave soon, but then again ..." I glanced at the door and frowned.

"You literally have nothing to worry about," she assured me as we walked inside.

Later, Karla dropped by my desk, her backpack filled with all the contents of her desk. It looked unwieldy on her small frame. "I'm getting out of here. Just had my exit interview."

"How'd it go?" I asked.

She bit her lip for a moment, then said, "I may have said a few things."

"Good for you, friend," I said as I stood and gave her a hug. "Good for you."

"Well, you've got my email," she said.

I motioned over to my cell phone in its shiny blue case. "My husband just hooked gmail up to my phone. I'm modern now."

"All right," she said quietly. We'd agreed there'd be no fanfare when she left; she wanted to slip out the door, turn in her badge at the main office, and be on her way.

"See you later," I whispered, then waved as she turned and walked quietly down the aisle of cubicles and out the door.

My cubicle was generous by modern standards. Tall walls enclosed most of my work area. It even contained storage drawers and a filing cabinet. The whole of my guts seemed to drop when I looked around it and realized that — without Karla around — it was going to be my bunker, the only indoor place I could belong at work. I'd continue taking my walks on my own, though, to geek out over the new tech.

I'd ignored Mary, an older woman with gorgeous long hair — white mixed with gray — who sat across from me, for a few months, though I doubted she had noticed. Although she'd been assigned to mentor me, she was likely too busy peppering the newbie she favored with assignments — a newbie who looked like she did, only younger — so that the newbie would look busy according to our odd timekeeping algorithms. Karla and I had been the orphans of the group; aside from my one direct assignment, we were dependent on others farming work out to us. Our manager, Christian, didn't concern himself with workflows unless big deadlines loomed, and thus work was currently unbalanced throughout the group, with some of us busy, and others like me and Karla, not so much.

I sighed deeply. I had cleanup to do from the big project I'd just finished, and then what? It was hard to concentrate on anything, and I had no idea what tasks should be done first or how to do them. I hadn't recovered from the burnout from the sixty-hour weeks I'd worked before the deadline the previous Friday, and there was no one to ask for direction. More reliable staff members were away, and I wasn't about to talk to Mary.

The last time I'd been at Mary's desk, needing assistance, she'd cracked up laughing at something on her computer screen. I asked her what was so funny, and she said, "Oh, just a joke." I waited a beat, then asked, "Are you going to share it with me?" and she said, "I can't." She just kept on laughing. I had a suspicion that I was somehow what she thought was so funny, though I didn't understand why, and the accompanying unease in the pit of my stomach didn't let up until I stood and walked outside to escape the sound of her laughter.

After that, I didn't talk to anyone else in the department unless it was at a staff meeting.

When Karla joined our group, I invited her to have lunch with me, and to my ultimate surprise, we became friends. We both hated working there; she had a hellish commute, and I was way too sensitive to the bad vibes. We were able to laugh about the quirks and oddities of our workplace, though, and back up each other's observations on who was acting sketchy.

Management, including Christian, had made Karla's role seem extra-temporary, emphasizing her contractor status and literally putting her in the corner of our office — not even at a proper desk or cubicle — even though the newbie Mary favored and I wore the same type of badge as Karla did. Some contractors there had worked for decades, nonstop, and HR had assured me at orientation that I was being hired for the long haul. I wasn't sure what distinguished any one contractor from the others.

This was why Karla had looked extra-happy when she gave notice.

"You can't put Karla in the corner," I said to her then.

She had nodded, smiling.

A few hours after Karla escaped, I received an Outlook meeting request from Christian for the next morning. This was unusual; he typically dropped by my desk to provide short assignments or talk about what I needed to work on next.

I relaxed at the sight of the time carved out of my quickly emptying schedule on Outlook. Perhaps we would talk about a new assignment, and, in the privacy of his office, I could ask him for a real mentor for the next project.

With something new to look forward to, the fog lifted; for the rest of the day, I arranged files — virtually and actually — according to what made sense to me, to wrap up my old project. By 4 p.m. I was amazed at how much I'd done. Perhaps I didn't need more time to work on my last assignment. Perhaps I could immerse myself in the new project right after my meeting with Christian.

☙

Walking up the hill to work the next day, I tripped on the sidewalk twice before I realized I was dragging my feet. Grateful for my sense of balance, but unhappy about relegating myself to my cube for the next four months — which I felt I needed to do in order to show the outside world that I was a consistent and reliable employee — I knew I had to power through the negativity.

Things will get better, I told myself. *This meeting will make everything come together.*

Ten o'clock couldn't come fast enough. Christian led a staff meeting every day at 9:15, and first I had to sit through that and listen to Mary and her pinched-face sidekick describe the project they were collaborating on. None of my colleagues requested assistance with their tasks that day, so I remained mute. (I typically volunteered to collaborate with team members at these meetings, even though they usually ignored me, just to seem motivated and "part of the team.") Christian announced that Karla had left, and everyone (except me) looked around, seeming to be surprised that her former work station was now an unused computer on top of a table in the corner.

Christian made changes to the whiteboard, erasing tasks that were completed, adding others that needed to be done, while the meeting took place. He was a curious figure, young and thin, with short, blond hair and a perpetual reddish five o'clock shadow. Christian wore fitted pants or jeans every day with button-down long-sleeved plaid shirts and funky shoes that looked like they came from a haute couture bowling alley; the cut of the pants made his legs look skinny and his feet enormous.

I approached him at the whiteboard after the meeting and asked, "Good morning. Is there anything I need to bring to our meeting?" The raspiness of my voice surprised me. I supposed that was the result of not talking to anyone except my husband that morning.

"What?" he asked, and paused his hand in mid-erase. "No, just yourself. Maybe a notebook," he added.

I retreated to my desk, where the minutes ticked by, until it was time for our meeting. Clutching my recycled-paper notebook and black PaperMate pen, I knocked on the fake-wood door and turned the knob when Christian called, "Come in."

He motioned for me to close the door and to sit opposite him in a dingy green chair on a wooden base, then leaned forward onto his elbows, tented his fingers, closed his eyes, and sighed.

I sat, flipped to a fresh page of my notebook, uncapped my pen, and waited.

"We need to talk about the end of your contract," he said. His voice echoed throughout his small office crammed with shelves, books, and papers. Diffused sunlight streamed in through the 1950s single-glazed windows he'd cranked open to let in the fresh air.

"What?" I asked, tilting my head as my heart thudded.

"The end of your contract."

My back stiffened, and I looked at him, slowly comprehending what he'd said. "Oh, so *that's* what we're doing. When?" I sputtered, then took in a big breath.

"A week from today."

I gasped, then took a deep breath to recover. A flush of adrenaline flowed through my body, and I regained command of my thoughts.

"What about vacation days?" I asked. I'd been saving up for an out-of-town wedding a few months away, and Christian had already approved that time off. Of course he had.

"Um, you don't get paid for vacation, but we do honor sick days between now and your last day of work." He fidgeted with a paper on his desk, on top of his giant desk calendar that was covered in scrawls.

"I have nearly a week's worth of sick time banked," I muttered, then looked up to meet his eyes. "Looks like I'm going to be sick for the next few days." I wasn't about to sequester myself in that cube and look for odds and ends to keep myself busy if I didn't have to.

I looked down at my notebook and the pen in my shaking hand, still poised to take notes for my next assignment, then lowered the notebook to my lap. After taking another breath, I felt some tension escape from my chest that I hadn't realized I'd been carrying.

Christian remained quiet, bowed his head, and allowed me to collect my thoughts.

Through the shock, I realized that I was no longer angry about having to work in the midst of chaos, no longer hiding away and hoping no one else would be rude to me, no longer sentenced to eating lunch by myself because Karla wasn't there anymore. Every exhale made me feel lighter, and once I started smiling, I couldn't stop.

Christian missed much of my reaction. He concentrated on a document on his desk, avoiding my gaze.

"What about our benefits?" I asked. We'd signed up for health insurance and benefits through them instead of using what my husband's employer offered. I never would have bothered with that, had I known.

He balked, then turned to his computer and clicked his mouse a few times. "I'm not sure."

My burst of laughter could no longer be contained. I shook my head and said, "You call someone into your office to *lay them off*, you ought to know the answer to a question like that." It took some effort not to call him "Kid." Christian's wide eyes told me that he was far out of his depth and didn't know how to act around me. He had probably anticipated tears, not laughter.

This job, all eight months of it, wouldn't look so bad on my resume. All I had to do was say I worked there until my contract ended. This was the ultimate "Get Out of Jail Free" card, because it was no one's fault when an organization ran out of money to pay its contractors, right?

I'd never been so happy about that weird blue strip on my swipe card with CONTRACTOR in white font, all caps.

Infused with a lightheaded feeling of relief, I thanked Christian for his time, took the packet with information about my "transition" from him, glided to my desk, shut down the computer, picked up my lunchbag and purse, and quietly made my way down the aisle and out the office door. *I'm following in Karla's footsteps*, I realized as my smile grew wider.

The familiar walk to the parking lot was bursting with life, where hummingbirds zipped among hibiscus flowers and Western Scrub-Jays chirped. A line of tall pine trees filtered the sun's rays as I walked down the hill. I laughed when I realized I hadn't noticed any of that for a long time.

The whole world was alive again, and so was I.

BURNING MAN

James Ferry

Vendome Street, being staggered, cut through Silver Lake and Echo Park at different points, two "ends" of the same road. Why city planners hadn't simply named one end Vendome and the other something else was anybody's guess. People got disoriented. Adobe homes, most of them occupied to the hilt, abutted one another, all of them in flux with encroaching gentrification, rent control now a thing of the past. The National Film Registry, stalwart as they were, had managed to retain the Music Box Steps, the very spot where Laurel and Hardy shot their famous short in 1932. They say it was a remake of sorts: a follow-up to *Hats Off*, which they'd shot five years earlier, only instead of lugging a piano up the steps, they lugged a washing machine. That film mysteriously vanished; it hasn't been seen since 1927. Recently, the hipsters moved in and quickly got priced out. Stucco structures of various sizes were rehabbed into "flats" occupied with faces morphing mostly from brown to white, imperturbable into ashen and gaunt.

A former flatmate of mine, an adjunct, had OD'd in the back hall. Air, smelling like death, hung in the whole house, and the bathroom was littered with paraphernalia and other ephemeral items. (Judging the purity of the product had become like guessing the motives of a friend: hard to gauge and discernable only in hindsight.) We sanitized his rigs and tidied up the place before calling the coroner. Among his belongings, I found some scuffed up books, the pages of which were heavily annotated: *Justine* by de Sade, *Naked Lunch*, and *Confessions of an Opium Eater*. I liked the last best because the hero is irredeemable. (De Quincey lived a dope fiend, died a dope fiend. At least he was consistent.) He had been a very pedantic junkie; his books were well organized and cross-referenced with other obscure publications, many of which were academic screeds garnering few, if any, citations.

When the long days of summer came, usually we could get out of bed before dusk fell. When we met at the club, our blemishes could be obscured. The black light and dinginess acted like an equalizer: if we all looked equally shitty, then we all looked similarly cool. Three men to a stall we'd scrape our bags and lift our feeble arms toward our noses. The (adulterated) powder stung us, but soon our bodies warmed. Our spinal cords felt as though they were wrapped in cotton wool. The momentum of the evening brought us through back alley doorways, bypassing velvet ropes and into green rooms and sound booths, where we would light cigs and watch the show from behind the glass. When we returned to the street, the vendors had already packed up their carts (not that eating was at all desirable). If our landlord was seen leaving the building, we'd hide in the alley until he was safely out of view. Or if Sanjay's sister came over from Los Feliz to ask her brother for a fix, we'd gawk at her from the safety of the shadows. She'd be waiting for him, her dope sickness defined by the sweat beads on her brow. Her brother always teased her before he complied, and I leaned on the railing looking at her. Her skinny arms swung as she swayed side to side, and her pin eyes glowed in the oily flame of her Zippo.

Every night I would sit on the stoop, pretending not to wait for her. Always my laptop was at the ready so I could seem to be engrossed. When she appeared on the street my heart palpitated. I ran to the bathroom, settled my stomach and retained my composure. This happened night after night. I simply didn't have the nerve to engage her unaccompanied or sober. I had barely spoken to her, except for a few drug-addled words, and yet her aura was like something that would have spooked Walter Benjamin.

Her image haunted me even in contexts unconducive to lovesickness. On the evenings when my roommate had a gig, I would have to lug equipment into the van. We drove to the strip, stopping for stumbling hipsters and heedless prostitutes, the homeboys in their khakis, the bums pushing their shopping carts, the Valley Girls slumming in their Priuses, the exhaust sputtering as the needle dipped precariously below E. These eclecticisms converged in a single sensation for me: I imagined that I'd lost all perspective and that I'd never die while the sun was shining. Her name sprang to my lips at inopportune moments: sound checks, situations that simply did not warrant it. My speech was often full of garble (I could not help myself), and at times a knot in my stomach seemed to spread to my larynx, my lymph nodes. Clearly I had no future. I didn't know whether I would live long enough to impress her, and if I impressed her, how I could hide my crippling insecurity. But my body was like a marionette's, and her words and gestures were like a puppeteer's handiwork.

One night I went into the back hall where my roommate had died. It was a dry, smoggy evening, and some stray cat was clearly in heat. Laptop balanced precariously on my knee and my button fly loose, I kept scrolling through porn, determined not to settle. Clickbait was always so promising, but the product left too much to be desired. Some familiar image kept provoking me. The Cars were on Spotify ("Moving in Stereo"), and I was thankful that I still felt virile.

All my innards seemed primed for effusion and, feeling as though I were about to burst, I gripped my organ tightly with the tremolo, "O God! O God!"

"Jesus Christ!"

She'd taken the Lord's name in vein [sic]. I was so embarrassed when I saw her standing over me that I just about wanted to die. She asked me if I was going to Burning Man. I forgot whether or not going was a cool thing to do. It would be a dope-ass festival; she said she was hot in the biscuit to go.

"What, like, you can't make it or something?" I asked.

When she spoke she toyed with a hangnail she had. She could not go, she said, because there was a conflict: the festival coincided with Fashion Week in New York. Rumor had it that Terry Richardson wanted to meet with her. Her brother and two other guys were fighting over the last Pabst, and I was still balancing my laptop. Shifting her gaze away from me, she pulled out one of her Parliaments. The flame from her Zippo burned orange and blue, lighting up her pin eyes and, flickering, nearly singed the ends of her Bettie Page bangs.

"If I go," I said, buttoning my fly, "I'll buy you some kind of trinket or something, I swear."

"It's strictly a gift economy," she said, staring off. "Burning Man supports itself on love."

What an unconscionable jackass I felt like after saying that to her! Of course one did not *purchase* anything at Burning Man. One acquired. It was spiritual. The whole idea was to immunize oneself against market dependency, to remove the proverbial toll booths from the communal road of human existence, to cleanse the soul, to *decommodify*. I knew this … or I'd overheard somebody talking about it once at the Silver Lake Lounge, which pretty much amounted to the same thing.

For consecutive days, my eyes seemed to sting. The air conditioner dripped like a sieve, the coyotes howled as though the mountains had gone meatless. I could barely roadie without feeling the Burn; even tuning a guitar made me quiver with anticipation. The syllables of the words "Burning Man" reverberated through every note. I labored under the lights while my skin exfoliated, my whole life revolving around a large wooden effigy.

I put in for the week off. My boss was pissed and hoped it was not just some hipster affair. I tuned a few guitars, taped the wires down so nobody tripped. I watched my boss's face pass from irritability to indignation; he hoped I was about to die. I could barely stand the monotony of the road, the pack-up, the clean-up, the leaving for the next show. I was fearful of heights, could hardly lift a hundred pounds. I had specious knowledge of electrical equipment and, as of late, I'd been having some discomfort with my lower lumbar.

I felt obliged to remind my boss that I'd put in for the following week off. He was fussing with the mic stand, looking for the Sani Flush, and he answered me brusquely: "*What the fuck?*"

As he was in a mood, I decided to leave him a simple reminder, a sticky note would do. I felt the van was in bad juju and jaunted quickly toward the green room. The air was rank with mildew and the guy from the opening act was cooking up a shot.

When I went home to pass out, my landlord was futzing with the locks. An eviction notice was stabbed to the door like it was Luther's Disputation. I sat on the curb for some time and felt numbness and antipathy welling up inside me. At least we'd gotten all the gear out. None of us had any illusions about staying here very long and, admittedly, the place was starting to stink something awful. Those dank, warm, cluttered rooms reeked of death, the whole place felt like a pitstop on the junkie express, and I was hardly sentimental about it. There was always another flat. I made my way back to the club. I went from room to room looking for her, hoping to pretend to find her serendipitously, but she was never there. From behind the green room glass, I watched the band perform, some imitation Stooges-cum-Strokes kind of a thing, and then I saw her. I may have stood there for an hour, seeing nothing but that nymph-like figure, those long bony limbs swaying, stark and ambient in the black light, chain-smoking her Parliaments, orange and blue illuminating her pin eyes. I passed out.

I woke up to Billy, the lighting boy, going through my pockets. He was a runt, probably nineteen or something, too young to be so strung out, and I smacked his hands away and cuffed him one upside the head. He fixed his hair and grinned. Such a circumstance was hardly unusual and everybody knew the rules. Raiding was de facto tolerated, provided that one succeeded stealthily and without resorting to immorality (deployment of children and girlfriends, for instance, was strictly verboten). It was like *Bless the Beasts and Children*; if you could make it out of the cabin with the bull buffalo, then you were good. Otherwise it was a chamber pot full of piss in the face.

The band was droning on beyond all sanity and reason, and my boss still hadn't given me the go-ahead. I was half hoping that his liver would finally give out and that would be the end of it, but naturally my luck was never that good. "Sit down," I said to Billy. "I think I got at least two bumps here somewhere."

Billy said: "I don't think you're gonna make it to the desert, dude."

At midnight my boss came ambling through the door. He was an unmanageable drunk twenty-four hours a day, asleep or awake, thus I knew this would be akin to Custer's Last Stand. He was grumbling to himself and wielding a Fender Jaguar like an errant knight without any virtues.

"I need to talk to you," I said.

"*What the fuck?*"

It wasn't as though he'd forgotten. Lord knows none of us would remember our names if we hadn't had them tattooed somewhere on our bodies. It was that my request never registered to begin with.

I seethed with anger. "This. Is. Not. Negotiable."

"We're booked for next week! Don't forget Leif Garrett!"

I could feel a tendon pop in my hand as I clenched my fists.

Billy said to him sardonically: "Can't you just let him go? It's not like he can roadie worth a shit."

My boss told me to go fuck myself. He said he believed in the old adage, "*Think you're running and you escape yourself. Shortest way round is the longest way home.*" He asked me where in the hell I was "so hot in the biscuit" to go and, when I ignored him, he asked me if I had ever considered celebrating something ordinary instead of just miring myself in "philosophical realism." As I walked out the door, I could see, out of the corner of my eye, that he had Billy by the lapels and was sputtering in his face, "*They left and loved and laughed and lived!*" I checked my pockets for my last balloon. No, Billy (poor kid) had not absconded with it.

As I cruised down Sunset toward Cahuenga, I couldn't help but feel the thrum of the city. I'd heard somewhere that all cities have a particular "urban pulse," which captures the particular patterns of behavior that tend to manifest in any given locale. How on earth to efficiently transport, house, educate, employ, and entertain an ever-increasing number of bodies on a daily basis? Spatial and temporal variations of activity, a collection of *pulses*, can be harnessed and documented for the purposes of ongoing urban development.

Patterns I could accept. Patterns occur because we have a tendency to repeat the same behaviors and then we formulate expectations based on the results. But how bored would God — or whatever arbiter of the universe — have to be to descend upon our puny, individual lives? In Los Angeles people love to say, "Everything happens for a reason." I find it interesting that the storyteller always saves this platitude till the end, using it to punctuate some predigested tale about a life that could have been.

I read the back of my Burning Man ticket and realized that it was a disclaimer. I might die at the event and, if I did, it would be my fault exclusively. Apparently it's perilous and, although it's not well publicized, people die every year in the desert. Serious bodily injury may occur. Nearly everyone around you will be intoxicated, some of whom will be operating incredibly dangerous and highly experimental machinery designed to be maximally destructive. There are rapes and other forms of assault. People may kill you or, in a momentary lapse of exaggerated merriment, you may kill yourself. If you have any kind of medical condition that could result in an emergency, you're fucked. You're a million miles away from the help that you need.

All of this printed, in block lettering, on the back of the ticket.

I drove onward through Barstow, a seemingly endless stretch of desert en route to Black Rock. It was a moonless night, and I'd tapped my balloon in Reno (not killing it, just getting by). At last I could see the lights of the tents of a million other Burners off in the distance. I kept driving, but I was kicking up dust and seeming not to get any closer. The lights I saw simply didn't match up with any particular direction, and the abundancy of stars were all but useless; I didn't know which way was north. I kept driving in circles, but everything looked the same. It was like being on one of those endless loops off the highway, where you can see the Walmart or whatever, but you just can't get there, can't seem to find the right off ramp, the *one* exit or jug handle. After an interminable delay, I finally reached the greeters at Black Rock Gate. How could I have missed the kiosks along the way, they wanted to know. I was answerless. I passed quickly through the gate, handing my ticket to a gnarly looking hippie. I hadn't brought any money, thus I was a little nervous about food and water and shelter and sunblock. Everyone seemed to be wearing some sort of rickshaw-style hat, too. Smart. A few hours on the playa and I was bound to be burnt. People ducked in and out of crudely made tents and danced animatedly with glow sticks and other things that glowed.

The playa was a modern-day Dust Bowl, a howling wilderness. I could barely open my eyes, when suddenly a body-painted youth on a unicycle went by. I flagged him down and introduced myself. He claimed to be an emissary of Neptune, left behind to preside over the lake since the ancient sea had receded. I asked him if the dust was always this bad. "The rock abides," he said, "sea-born emperor of the dust." He explained that we were grooving on a dry bed of an ancient lake that gets resurfaced and smoothed most winters by wind and water, resulting in a vast and very, very flat expanse. "It's so flat," he said, "that it causes mirages."

"Mirages?"

"Yeah, distances in particular can be hard to judge."

I experienced that problem on the way in, I explained. "I kept thinking I was on my way toward the camp and then I realized that I wasn't getting any closer. You know that feeling where you can see where you want to go, but you just can't get there?"

With that he de-cycled and stepped toward me, took me by the wrists and inverted my arms and inspected them. "You've been on a drug loop," he said, looking at me real shaman-like. "You've been caught in a repetitive pattern, which you don't even recognize as a repetitive pattern, a metaphoric loop in which you're centripetally pulled toward sameness and again-ness. You know this is happening, you may even scold yourself for it, yet you fail to connect it with the core problem."

"What … what *is* it?"

"I think you know."

With that he mounted his unicycle and pedaled off into the darkness.

I wanted to behold *the Man*, if only to see the effigy around which so many people coalesce every year, but I didn't make it. I met a woman named Sara: dressed all in white, a top hat, heart-shaped glasses, and a Cheshire cat smile.

"Come and share your fears," she said, holding out a Sharpie.

"I don't think you have enough paper."

"Paper's too finite," she said. "The Closet is a love letter that never ends. When we run out of space we just build a new wing."

Her whole installation was an interactive outdoor closet, painted white and scrawled all over in black ink. *Not fitting in enough to be happy. Not being good enough for the ones that mean the most to me. Feeling wrong and feeling broken (but I know I'm not!).* It was her life's work, Sara explained. She'd been to an LGBTQ retreat and she was floored by the amount of history — oral history — that was being shared and left unrecorded. "I decided to collect their stories and document them," she said, "because too much had already been lost. We used to pretend to be straight and have kids, hiding who we were. Then the next generation came out and dealt with the backlash — Reagan barely mentioning AIDS and so many people dying. I wanted to build a big open closet that could hold all our hopes and fears, not metaphorically, but *literally*. I had trouble finding a carpenter who had the time, so I apprenticed and built it myself."

It was amazing: a sprawling apparatus, eight feet high and twenty feet long, replete with white clothing. There were chests of drawers too. Some contained photos of transgender people who'd been murdered. Other drawers had bottles of experimental cocktails that AIDS patients had consumed during the eighties, just trying to survive.

My initial fears concerning my lack of provisions turned out to be pointless. Within hours I'd been outfitted with a poncho and one of those hats, and I'd been given water, iced coffee, and enough fresh-squeezed lemonade to quench the nastiest thirst. I took in a blues concert and briefly joined a bluegrass community on bass. I began offering my roadie services (meager as they were) to any musician or technician I could find. There was always something new to explore and every door was open to me. Everyone was friendly, and every stranger had a story or a gift or both.

I found my way to *Pulse and Bloom*, where twenty lotuses of varying heights had pulse sensors mounted on the bases of their stems. I was joined briefly by a woman who was there to debut her own installation (a giant cloth-stitched vagina smeared in Vaseline; anyone who felt inclined could walk through, she said, and experience rebirth). When we placed our hands on the sensor, both the stem and the flower began to pulsate and glow. We smiled and watched as the beating hearts of all the participants — a collection of *pulses* — made the lotuses light up like fireflies.

Remembering with shame why I had come, I went over to one of the booths and examined the exquisite artwork: handmade bracelets and beaded necklaces that must have taken ages to construct; they were so elaborate. The woman must have labored over each and every one. She laughed heartily with her fellow Burners. I listened casually to their conversation.

"What do you want for it?"

"Oh, you can have it!"

"But I want to trade something, at least!"

"I don't need anything in return, really!"

"Are you sure?"

"Oh yes, I'm positive!"

Observing me, the young lady came over and handed me a bracelet. The look in her eye was empathic; she seemed genuinely interested in giving me something. I accepted humbly and thanked her. I wasn't used to this. I was used to slacked jaws and pinned eyes and cursory attention spans. How would I go back to Los Angeles, my life, my impending death?

I woke up at dawn on Sunday and stepped outside the tent. Half of the tents that were there the night before had vanished. Most of the art installations had been dismantled or burned. The iced coffee guy had departed, the lemonade girl was gone. The aerial dancers, the fire-eaters, the drum-circle warriors, no more. They'd left no trace. Just as I was growing accustomed to navigating it, the city was disappearing before my eyes. It was so unlike Silver Lake, where things disappear for myriad morbid reasons (displacement, disillusionment, destitution, death), but always with a sense of numbness and apathy.

I lingered on the playa, though I could feel it was time to go. Then I turned and began the long walk back toward the gate. I pulled my last balloon, the remnants, from my pocket and dropped it in the sand. The sun had come up and it was now completely light.

Gazing off into the desert I could feel myself as a human worthy of love and forgiveness; and my eyes welled with hope and tears.

With grateful acknowledgment to Sara von Roenn for her permission to mention the Opening the Closet art installation in this story, we encourage readers to support her GoFundMe campaign.

https://www.gofundme.com/get-the-closet-across-the-country

EDITION OF TEN

Abigail Walthausen

Paul liked to brag to neighbors about his plantings, in particular the fire-retardant trees — the scrub oaks and the cherries. But what these trees never ended up retarding was the dust that came up the side of the hill in the fire season whether fires burned or not. Ash smoke or dust, those dry months coated every leaf and weed.

He liked to brag to neighbors about the height of his corn, and Margaret wondered whether those same neighbors ever hoped for a bag of cobs to bring home and boil. But height or no height, Paul's corn never fruited well, the kernels stayed puckered without their summer sugars.

He bragged about the way the animals loved him and the furniture he built them in return. The birdfeeder was charming — it hung on an arm that could retract into the kitchen window with a little pulley system. Then, there on the counter, Margaret could fill its four separate little troughs with four different types of seeds and the little reservoir for hummingbird nectar as well. What she did not care for was the possum ladder that went right up to the attic from the sitting room. Paul wanted the critters to feel comfortable in the crawlspace in their eaves, but Margaret was sure that they were peeing up there. And the ladder would welcome more nests, and more baby possums would mean more possum pee. A wood frame house, she told Paul, can only absorb so much possum pee before there is rot.

He bragged least of all about his patronage — Hollywood directors, a well-known actress, a bookseller, a gallerist or two — but even though he bragged only about things made by his own hands, these brushes with fame set him glowing. When Margaret was in the studio with him, when she helped him tighten the press, when he peeled the paper from the block, a smugness surfaced on those days when gifts and help and invitations came in.

Sometimes that satisfaction was wholesome, and she savoured Paul as he looked right there in front of her, press-side, at the moments before a first printing. For weeks he would polish a woodblock, attend to it with delicate engraver's tools where other, lesser artists would hack away with gouges. And then, they'd translate his engravings from things of sawdust and scars, shadow and texture that only imply image, to something plainspoken, black and white. She beamed too at the way the ink looked crisp along the jagged edge of a mountain or the finest line, a scratch, made the wispy edge of a figure's thigh. And there was the bite that wood on paper made — they pressed and the pricey Japanese paper yielded.

Margaret did other work for Paul too, out of the studio. When she wrote his letters, responded to commissions, or invoiced galleries, the printing press haunted her. She missed it as she sat at the typewriter, each crisp black letter that she coaxed out of the agile modern machine a reminder of the real work, the greater work. This typing, it had once made Margaret her living — she'd worked downtown, a copywriter climbing the ranks. But now typing was not just words: it was shored up by a reserve of the little bricks of wood and the huge clamp and the hours and hours of studio time that whiled away while she typed and kept house and slept and waited to be called in for a hand.

Margaret stepped out to the mailbox for a moment —
it was early for anything to come, but she had her outgoing
letters and a clothespin. She could as easily have pinned
them up on her way out for errands, plenty of those today,
but she always liked to test the air first.

From around the bend came the sound of gravel and
dry leaves, then Martin talking loudly. "Well, Margaret,
tell Paul that it looks like Ingrid is getting her streetlamp
after all," he said from across the road, walking and winking, arm in arm with Isobel. "We'll have to see how many
helpless damsels are saved by this new addition." They
took their little exercise at this time and today, as always,
they were overdressed — him in a jacket too heavy for
the weather, her in a shawl — something from travels to
a place with scenic peasants — Hungary? Peru, maybe?
They were formal and bundled and Margaret did not care
for the way they took Paul's side about the streetlamp
without ever stopping to ask hers. Martin and Isobel had
learned from their particular type of marriage to count
on consensus, to have a co-conspirator. How nicely that
subtle fortification went together with the formal bundles
of their clothing!

Just because no one in the neighborhood liked that old
gossip Ingrid didn't mean that her fears were wrong. Up
here on the hill, Margaret could turn her head south and
see downtown, north and see Glendale. There was nothing
stupid about acknowledging that this was a big city.

The streetlamp was to be installed at the foot of Landa
Street Stairs. Margaret walked them every day, and when
she had occasion to walk them at night, alone, she soaked
up the frisson of Los Angeles — a metropolis that really
was as seedy and as noir as the films showed. And hobos
did come up into the hills to camp out too. Did Paul not
ever worry that she might be raped in the dark tunnel of

bougainvillea that the stairs made at night? Maybe it didn't occur to him or maybe he'd felt that frisson too and decided to protect it. Disaster and consequences. Wasn't too late for Margaret to come home with child — unspeakable idea, she knew, but she was one of seven and well aware of the violence of childbearing. Was it so awful for the moment of child-getting to be a brutal one too? Short fright compared to the lovely, long milky-sweet life of a baby. Her romance with Paul had been gentle always, but wasn't the other way the way it had been with all the cavemen?

Maybe it would be a better child than the one they weren't able to conceive because of the ethics of it. Dark-alley rapists would always leave their waifs, their orphans, their mongrel spawn somewhere, and those unfortunates would need help. She and Paul had talked before about taking in a child like that but gotten caught up in the way it might be marked by early hovels and abuses. But an urchin of the staircase might be born in their home, a place carefully shored up on the hillside "like a redwood dam," their poet-friend had said, with garden plots around it and a breeze that really was healthful even so close to the city. If Paul could father so tenderly a possum, a petrel, then there must be no limit to what he could tame to fit their little environment.

Martin and Isobel nodded their goodbyes and strode away on straight legs, in step as though ice dancing, and wearing dainty shoes even on this dusty road. They played bohemian, the professorial strand of that, but Martin worked at an office downtown and Isobel shopped there oftener than most others on the hill shopped at all. And she met Martin for lunch down there whenever her errands took the day. Did she take a taxi home if she became too loaded down with boxes for the streetcar? No wonder she didn't care about the lamp.

Margaret found a second clothespin on the mailbox, one she'd left out yesterday. She took it down and clipped it lightly on her fingertip. What a contraption it was. More wood and metal to leave a bloodless impression, but this one with all its force to press packed inside itself. Bloodless was too cruel a term, though, for the fields of dear white paper. She looked at her drained finger and thought of how she loved her own pale figure in Paul's art, of how much she loved all of Paul's art.

She popped inside and clipped the clothespin on the end of the table runner, a long strip of an old flour sack that she'd printed with a few of Paul's ruined blocks — ones that had suffered unfixable mistakes, or cracked with age, or had been rendered in linoleum, a more forgiving medium from which Paul had moved on.

She had used a dark green ink and stamped the blocks in a random order, shape, and size, alternating like a string of beads, irregular like turquoise chips. And there had been so much of this discarded work that Margaret only had to repeat the sequence twice to cover the five-foot sideboard. Well, she clipped the clothespin to the rumpled end of the runner, and from the first drawer she grabbed her market things: two string bags she stuffed into her purse and money for the Red Car. She sat on the stoop for a moment to dust off the soles of her feet before slipping them into moccasins. She didn't say goodbye to Paul — he'd been in the studio already for hours this morning and would want no disturbance. She shushed Horace's barks as she hustled him inside and closed the door.

She headed down the hill and startled when she saw the workmen on the stairs, as though she had wished that streetlamp into being. Martin and Isobel had warned her this was happening, though she had not expected it today! Why had she assumed they had classified news of a permit, that they knew what was coming down the pipeline in city government? They'd only just seen the lamp in person. Still, she felt the shame of guilt as though she had defied Paul and wished away the possums and the skunks that owned the land in the shadowy dusk. She defied Paul, and the rapists and waifs skittered off too. It was midday, but come night it would be just her and Paul and his complaints about the creeping city and light pollution and where are all the redwing blackbirds now?

"Good afternoon," she said to the electricians as she approached.

"Ma'am," they said back to her, and she slowed her descent to inspect their ladder, the pole, the excavation, the pit of cement. At the bottom of the stairs was a wooden crate, top off, with a glass globe nestled into some straw. Jumping the gun, she thought, with so much to be done before that nicety, that little bit of the domestic, could be screwed on.

Once she was down the stairs and around the corner, she remembered the canning supplies that she needed to get at the hardware store. There was no way she would carry a flat of Mason jars home with her on the streetcar. Back up the stairs she went to grab the push cart. Again, somehow, the workers startled her, though she had passed them only thirty seconds before.

"Back so soon?" one electrician said to her.

Margaret chuckled. "Forgot something at home," and nodded towards the shade as though the men would be able to make the connection between that big glass shade and the little glass bulbs of canning jars that it had called to mind. "You'll be at this a while, won't you?"

"Just making the street safer at night for ladies like you," he said.

"For ladies like you ..." began the other with a more joking tone, a crooked nod of the head, "I'd build another

Angel's Flight here, and one on every single hillside in this crazy neighborhood." He winked from beneath his helmet. "Ladies shouldn't have to climb a staircase like this day or night — then you could go out in your good shoes." He nodded at her turned-over moccasins. Margaret slid her purse back up her shoulder and opened her mouth as if to answer.

"You nut," put in the other worker. "Bunker's got to be three times as high as this hill. Or more!" He turned to Margaret but nodded towards his friend, "He'll use any line on the ladies."

"Well, my husband built a little funicular for our yard — just to give the groceries a hoist from the fire road to our front door. And that hill is maybe a quarter of this one here." Margaret was not sure what her point was, but she was emphatic.

The one in the helmet frowned. "Seems like maybe that husband of yours ought to just carry those bags up for you if that's all the hill you're talking about."

"Actually we have erosion, so it is a very steep one," she said because she didn't quite know how to say mind your business. Because her words were degrees more polite than her spiteful thoughts and because his frown still furrowed, she added, "and he was crippled in the war." Now the quality of his grimace changed — it lost its scolding irony and began to beam. Margaret also beamed because the war was a load of horseshit, it had been childhood meningitis and here was this fool with a brain full of fireworks, heart blowing a doodle-dandy kazoo all for a load of horseshit.

"God bless, ma'am," he said, "and we'll be here for the rest of the afternoon and tomorrow if you and the mister need a hand with anything, anything at all around the house."

"Not likely." She nodded a curt nod and started up the stairs, because all the sudden she had remembered how to say mind your own business. The war was a lie that she had thought of before but never used. Made it seem like her husband's handicap, that stiff leg and stiff arm, was something that happened to her rather than something she had elected in marrying a damaged man. Paul might have liked the lie to be true, because he was the sort, like most, who preferred to look more heroic than not.

He liked a little bombast, and his crippling annoyed him, made him a bit raw sometimes, but still he was mostly so sweet to her. He made a point of sketching her whenever she looked her best, and sometimes he sketched her and made her look a bit better. When he first took up printing, he made her little cards, little bookplates, a business card that said, "Margaret, Swell Gal." He didn't ask for help so much when they first moved into the cottage — she just saw when he was overwhelmed and stepped in, but over time that stepping in became expected. He would be home still, maybe waiting for a hand. She looked down the stairs again, and the workmen were back at the electrical wires, threading them.

Margaret was frozen at the hill's crest — now that she thought about it and now that she'd come up the stairs and gotten snarky with the workers, she knew she did not need the jars yet. Sure she was out of jars — Paul kept stealing the small ones to mix ink — but there was nothing for her to preserve at the moment but a bunch of lemons that were too bitter and fibrous for any other purpose. None of their fruit trees made anything great — the figs were wormy, though it was hard to see that wriggling life until they'd sat out on the counter for a day or two.

She didn't need the jars, or the push cart, and the men were not looking up the stairs at her, stalled, perversely wishing that she had worn the sort of shoes that would make her walk the walk that would make them look. She was stuck now on a landing between the ones she'd lied to and the one she'd lied about. Paul was probably in his studio touching up a block with an image of the L.A. River, a view under the Glendale bridge with two children and a horse playing in the water. Horses maybe, there was a paddock by there, but it was hobos who bathed under the bridge, not Paul et Virginie. Engraving the detail in the brickwork had taken him a week, but the water itself, with longer flowing ripples, he did this morning, and if she went back into the house now and he was inking up for a test run, odds would have it that she would run the press with him. He called her the captain when she turned the wheel for him, but she felt more like she was opening a vault that barely budged — or one that was a prank holding bewildering inventory — a single sheet of paper, black and white.

Paul had never done a portrait of her face alone. She knew that he could; he'd done a great series of composers for KECA. She wasn't sure how to ask for it, but she was somehow certain she would feel better about things if Paul stopped to read her face the way he had the face of Jan Sibelius or of Claude Debussy. How many different portraits and photographs had he looked at to arrive at a single block for each man? Margaret had appeared in plenty of Paul's art, nestled in amongst scenery, but these men, these composers, faced out of an inky black plane and had nothing beneath the chin to worry over.

Margaret peered into the kitchen window to see if the house was empty, if Paul was still in the studio. Horace, a thick dog with no neck who himself looked like a great boxy skull, disembodied, heard her. Horace threw himself, trunk-like paws first, at the front door. Such a thud. Now

Paul hollered from downstairs and Margaret supposed she would go in because she could not run off and hide now that the dog was barking too.

A breeze flew through the kitchen with two doors open at once. It was the same breeze that carried dust up the hill, but this one brought Margaret and Paul into the space near the sink where their gazes met and hovered over Horace, who'd backed into the center of the room. The basement door closed and floorboards creaked, and when Paul was close enough, he brushed Margaret's hair aside and used his thumbs as if to polish her cheekbones. Margaret's breath left her for a moment as he stroked and measured, but she coughed out a little practical attention.

"Did you finish the bridge?" Margaret asked, sorry she had snuck off, sorry she had lied. "Do you need help with a test print?"

Paul nodded and moved his thumbs to the place where her forehead domed up from the hairline. The thrill of having her measurements taken. A grit of dust was in her sweat, the gentlest abrasion under his touch. "Oh, Margaret," Paul said, "if you had ten sisters, wouldn't the world be a happier place?"

BIOGRAPHIES

Sara Chisolm

Sara Chisolm was born and raised in the City of Angels. She still resides here with her two young children, who insist on being called by the weird pet names that their mother has bestowed upon them. When Sara isn't teaching small children, she is chugging bubble tea or coffee while frequenting the cultural enclaves of her hometown. She is interested in learning about different cultures and languages. She lives by the mantra that "one more book isn't enough books," so she continues to buy more. She enjoys writing speculative fiction based in urban settings.

Nick Duretta

Nick Duretta is a writer based in Pasadena, California. His career has encompassed a wide range of activities, from managing communication programs for Fortune 500 corporations to writing textbooks and screenplays. He has also conducted writing and oral presentation workshops and spoken at several international communication conferences. He is now focused on writing fiction. (His current project: a series of mystery novels.) When not hunched over his keyboard, he is out walking in the Southern California mountains and hills, enjoying his favorite pastime.

James Ferry

James Ferry did his MFA at Goddard College, his MA at UMass, and he's currently at URI, working on his PhD. His work has appeared in *Academe Magazine*, *The Fiddleback*, *Pitkin Review*, *Heavy Feather Review*, *Citron Review*, and the *Hamilton Stone Review*, among others. He currently teaches college English courses to male offenders preparing to reenter society. A lifelong itinerant bachelor, he remains, at forty-five, single and childless. Though little about him could be called permanent, he can always be found at www.swirlsinthenegativespace.com.

Jude-Marie Green

Jude-Marie Green is a writer of genre (science fiction and fantasy, plus the occasional horror) fiction. She lives in Southern California amid palm trees, orange trees, avocado trees, roses, and birds. Lots of birds.

She is a fan of long standing. Her first convention was in 1977 at the Los Angeles Airport Marriott. She attends many conventions, including NorWesCon in Seattle where she is frequently a panelist and professional author as part of the Fairwood Writers Workshop. Find her online at: judemarie.wordpress.com.

Nolan Knight

Nolan Knight is a fourth generation Angeleno whose short fiction has been featured in various publications including Akashic Books, *Thuglit*, *Crimespree Magazine*, *Shotgun Honey* and *Needle*. He is a former staff writer for Los Angeles' biggest music publication, the *L.A. Record*. His debut novel *The Neon Lights Are Veins* was published by 280 Steps in 2017. He currently resides in Long Beach. Peep more at NolanKnight.com.

Gabi Lorino

Gabi Lorino started off life as a Tampeño, but now that she's reached the five-year mark in the City of Angels, she is officially an Angeleno. Finally, this place is starting to make sense!

Ms. Lorino writes stories that feature socially awkward women who occasionally interact with men. Her tales are based on her 20+ years in the dating world and hilarious stories told by friends, sisters, and strangers in public places. Gabi is a proud member of Generation X, and she's heard more than once that her characters "act a bit younger than they are" and maybe "need an attitude adjustment," which makes her love them even more!

Axel Milens

Born and raised in France, Axel Milens is now a proud American writer, husband, and father. He lives in the Hollywood Hills with his wife, his four boys, and a dog named Maybe (finally, a girl). Axel is working on a collection of short stories about the brave and sometimes tragic souls who survive, love, and die under the Southern California sun.

Allison Rose

Allison Rose is a novelist and screenwriter from Los Angeles. *Tick*, the first in her young adult science fiction series, tackles themes of mental illness, artistry, and violence. It has been followed by *Vice*, part two of the Tick Series. While Allison's stories vary in genre, her focus centers on the struggles of complex female characters.

Cody Sisco

Cody Sisco is the author of speculative fiction that straddles the divide between plausible and extraordinary. His Resonant Earth Series includes two novels thus far, *Broken Mirror* and *Tortured Echoes*, and a short story prequel, *Believe and Live*. The third novel in the series, *Altered Bodies*, will be published in 2019.

Cody is a 2017 Los Angeles Review of Books / USC Publishing Workshop Fellow. He is also a co-organizer of the Los Angeles Writers Critique Group. His start-up, BookSwell, makes the book scene in L.A. easier to navigate, introduces readers to new writing, and weaves together digital and real-life literary experiences. Find out more at: www.bookswell.club

C. Gregory Thompson

C. Gregory Thompson, a Pushcart Prize nominee, writes fiction, nonfiction, plays, and memoir. His work has appeared or is forthcoming in *The Maine Review*, *STORGY Magazine*, *Writers Resist*, *Five:2:One*, *Cowboy Jamboree*, *Full Grown People*, *The Offbeat*, *Printers Row Journal*, and *Reunion: The Dallas Review*. His work also appears in this anthology and *Writers Resist: The Anthology 2018*. He was named a finalist in the Tennessee Williams/New Orleans Literary Festival's 2015 Fiction Contest. He earned an MFA in Creative Writing and Writing for the Performing Arts at the University of California, Riverside/Palm Desert.

A.S. Youngless

A.S. Youngless has been passionate about writing since her childhood. She runs the Graphic Novel Book Club for elementary school students in the hope of sharing her love of writing with the next generation. "For Hire" is her first published story. She lives in beautiful Los Angeles with her husband, son, cat, fish, and hermit crab named Spider.

Abigail Walthausen

Abigail Walthausen lives in Los Angeles, where she writes and teaches.

MADE IN L.A. WRITERS

Made in L.A. Writers is a collaborative of Los Angeles-based authors dedicated to nurturing and promoting indie fiction. This 2019 volume is the second of the annual *Made in L.A.* anthology series. While our styles, themes, and story locales differ, our work is both influenced and illuminated by our hometown and underpinned by the extraordinary, multifaceted, and often surreal culture and life in the City of Angels.

As indie authors, we face formidable challenges: fragmented audiences, intense competition in a crowded market, and traditional publishers' deep pockets.

If you enjoyed this book, please leave a review. Rave about us to your friends. Find us online and tell us how our stories made you feel. We're looking for connection; we hope to hear from you.

www.madeinlawriters.com

ACKNOWLEDGMENTS

"Luigi's Song" by Jude-Marie Green first appeared in *For the Oceans* in 2011.

"Two Kings" by C. Gregory Thompson first appeared in *Offbeat Literary Magazine, Volume 16* in 2016.

"Mouth Bay" by Nolan Knight first appeared in *Crimespree Magazine Issue 66* in 2017.

CPSIA information can be obtained
at www.ICGtesting.com
Printed in the USA
FSHW011602200319
56525FS